"Do you do this often?"

"Meet men by swooning into their arms?" Annie asked, struggling for normalcy. "No, as a matter of fact, you're my first."

He gave her an assessing look. "You're pregnant."

He said it calmly, but to her it sounded like an accusation, and she bristled. As an unwed mother-to-be, she bristled a lot lately.

"Really?"

The stranger looked up at her for the first time, really seemed to look into her eyes and see who she was. Annie didn't think she'd ever seen bluer eyes.

But there was more. He had the look of a man who did and said whatever occurred to him. Everything in her wanted to like him. He looked… well, nice. And that was even more dangerous than his undeniable sex appeal. The way he took charge so naturally. The way he was poised, down on one knee before her, like a knight asking a lady for her scarf to wear into battle.

Dear Reader,

May has to be one of the most beautiful months of the year. Having been trapped indoors for the cold, dark winter, I love taking long walks and discovering new shops and restaurants that have opened in New York. And everywhere I turn, multicolored flowers line street medians; the sidewalks are flooded with baby carriages and the bridal salons lining Madison Avenue feature gowns that would make any woman feel like a princess.

As our special tribute to May, we've gathered romances from some of your favorite writers and from some pretty stellar new voices. Raye Morgan's BOARDROOM BRIDES continues with *The Boss's Special Delivery* (SR #1766). In this classic romance, a pregnant heroine finds love with her sworn enemy. Part of the FAIRY-TALE BRIDES continuity, *Beauty and the Big Bad Wolf* (SR #1767) by Carol Grace shows how an ambitious career woman falls for a handsome recluse. The next installment in Holly Jacobs's PERRY SQUARE miniseries, *Once Upon a Princess* (SR #1768), features a private investigator who's decided it's time a runaway princess came home…to him! Finally, two single parents get a second chance at love, in Lissa Manley's endearing romance *In a Cowboy's Arms* (SR #1769).

And be sure to come back next month when Patricia Thayer and Lilian Darcy return to the line.

Ann Leslie Tuttle
Associate Senior Editor

The BOSS'S Special DELIVERY

RAYE MORGAN

Published by Silhouette Books

America's Publisher of Contemporary Romance

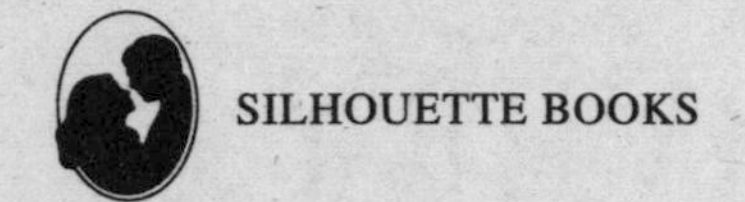

ISBN 0-373-19766-7

THE BOSS'S SPECIAL DELIVERY

This edition published by arrangement with Harlequin Books S.A.

Visit Silhouette Books at www.eHarlequin.com

Printed in U.S.A.

Books by Raye Morgan

Silhouette Romance

Roses Never Fade #427
Promoted—To Wife! #1451
The Boss's Baby Mistake #1499
Working Overtime #1548
She's Having My Baby! #1571
A Little Moonlighting #1595
†*Jack and the Princess* #1655
†*Betrothed to the Prince* #1667
†*Counterfeit Princess* #1672
††*The Boss, the Baby and Me* #1751
††*Trading Places with the Boss* #1759
††*The Boss's Special Delivery* #1766

Silhouette Books

Wanted: Mother
"The Baby Invasion"

Royal Nights

Silhouette Desire

Embers of the Sun #52
Summer Wind #101
Crystal Blue Horizon #141
A Lucky Streak #393
Husband for Hire #434
Too Many Babies #543
Ladies' Man #562
In a Marrying Mood #623
Baby Aboard #673
Almost a Bride #717
The Bachelor #768
Caution: Charm at Work #807
Yesterday's Outlaw #836
The Daddy Due Date #843
Babies on the Doorstep #886
Sorry, the Bride Has Escaped #892
**Baby Dreams* #997
**A Gift for Baby* #1010
**Babies by the Busload* #1022
**Instant Dad* #1040
Wife by Contract #1100
The Hand-Picked Bride #1119
Secret Dad #1199

†Catching the Crown
††Boardroom Brides
*The Baby Shower

RAYE MORGAN

has spent almost two decades, while writing over fifty novels, searching for the answer to that elusive question: Just what is that special magic that happens when a man and a woman fall in love? Every time she thinks she has the answer, a new wrinkle pops up, necessitating another book! Meanwhile, after living in Holland, Guam, Japan and Washington, D.C., she currently makes her home in Southern California with her husband and two of her four boys.

Chapter One

Annie Torres was going to faint. The signs were all there. Staring hard at her order pad, she tried to fight the feeling.

Just give me one more minute, she begged silently. *Just let me get into the break room.*

"Oh, wait," her customer was saying. "I think I want a side of fries with that. And can I get a serving of blue cheese dressing to go with the fries?"

The room was starting to turn, very slowly, but it was turning. She felt clammy. It was only a matter of seconds. Flipping her book closed, she started to step away, desperate to get to the break room.

"Miss? Wait a minute. I forgot about dessert. Do you have any of that great fresh peach pie today?"

It sounded like the woman was talking to her from the end of a tunnel. The words were echoing in her head and something was pounding in her ears. She had to get out of there. She tried to turn back, but it was too late. She was wilting like a rose in the hot summer sun. It was all over.

"Hey."

She opened her eyes. There were faces all around, staring down at her. Something in her wanted to laugh. They looked so funny. Then she realized she was lying on the floor of Millie's Café and it didn't seem so funny any longer.

Each face had a mouth and each mouth was moving but she couldn't tell what they were saying. She closed her eyes, wishing they would all go away and leave her alone. Her head was throbbing.

"I'll handle this."

Finally a deep, masculine voice stood out from the babble and she felt cool, strong hands probing for injuries and testing her reactions.

"Does anything hurt?" he asked her.

She shook her head and regretted it, because her head hurt like crazy. But it wasn't from hitting the floor, it was just a headache.

"Sorry," she muttered, trying to get up. "I'd better get back to work."

"Not likely." Suddenly she was being swung up into the arms of what had to be a fairly strong man.

"Hey," she said weakly, pushing back and trying to look up into his face.

"Just relax, honey," he said in a soothing voice. "I've got you."

"But I don't need getting," she protested, pushing ineffectively against his shoulder with her hands.

"Don't try to talk," he told her as he carried her through the crowded café. "You're obviously delirious."

He said it with a touch of humor, so she didn't take it seriously. He was probably trying to put her at ease about the situation. That wasn't necessary, because she didn't need his help. Much.

Though she had to admit, it felt so good to have such strong arms holding her. They were protective. Safe. And from what she could feel of him, pretty darn sexy. Which was exactly why she had to resist. If he would just put her down and let her get oriented…

But at least he knew where to take her. In just seconds she was in the break room and he was lowering her to the couch.

"Thank you, ladies," he said as someone handed him a damp cloth and a cup of water. "Just give us some room, please. Let me give her a quick examination. She'll be good as new in no time."

Bossy guy. As far as she was concerned, he could take that take-charge attitude and—

"Okay, Doctor," someone was saying.

Actually, it might have been Millie. Annie's eyes were closed and it was just too hard right now to open them and take a look. But if Millie was giving him permission to handle this, maybe she could relax a little. Millie was her boss, the owner of the café, and a thoroughly decent woman. Annie had come to realize lately that thoroughly decent people were hard to find and worth their weight in gold once discovered.

And he was a doctor, anyway. She relaxed a little more. She was more disposed to trust a doctor than she was to trust most men. After all, there was that Hippocratic oath thing.

"Just give a holler if you need anything," Millie added.

"Will do."

Annie finally got her eyes back open in time to see Millie leaving, and the very large man staying. As he continued to hover over her, he murmured something that made the others melt away. She appreciated that he'd dismissed the audience, because she'd had about enough of being the center of attention for a while.

Still, that meant she was alone with this man. Needing to reassert a little control of the situation, she pulled up to sit rather than staying down where he'd put her.

He didn't object. Instead, he put the cool cloth to her forehead, gave her a sip of water and then began taking her pulse. And finally her head cleared enough so that she could see straight again.

She looked him over, still groggy, head aching. Not bad, actually. He was handsome in a rugged, outdoorsy way—his thick hair dark and windblown looking, as though he'd just come in from chopping wood or chasing bears or something, and his eyes incredibly blue against his tanned skin. He looked familiar. She'd seen him in here at Millie's before. And she was pretty sure she'd seen him in years past. But it had only been a month since she'd come back to the Texas town of Chivaree and her ten or so years away had dimmed a lot of memories.

"How are you feeling?" he asked, studying her in a detached, clinical sort of way.

"Woozy."

He nodded and his eyes narrowed a bit. "Do you do this often?"

She struggled for normalcy. "Meet men by swooning into their arms?" she asked as impudently as she could manage. "No, as a matter of fact, you're my first."

He gave her an assessing look. "You're pregnant."

He said it calmly, but to her it sounded like an accusation, and she bristled. As an unwed mother-to-be, she bristled a lot lately.

"Really?" she responded quickly, straightening her shoulders as though she had to get ready for battle. "What was your first clue?"

He looked up and really met her dark gaze for the first time, really seemed to look into her eyes and see who she was. She had to stifle a shiver. She didn't think she'd ever seen bluer eyes.

But there was more. Something about him made her feel uncertain and a little self-conscious. He had the look of a man who did and said whatever occurred to him, without much worrying about what was appropriate to the occasion. If he saw something about her he liked...or didn't like...he was likely to be quite frank about it. And he proved she'd read him right with his next statement.

"You're also a smart aleck," he said dryly.

Still defensive, Annie stared right back at him. She had to make sure men like this knew she couldn't be intimidated. She'd had a lot of experience at this sort of thing lately. Learning how to protect herself by being a bit caustic hadn't come naturally, but she was learning.

"If I want character analysis, I'll go see a psychologist."

The corners of his mouth twitched. She wasn't sure if it was with humor or a quick irritation. Either way was okay with her—just so long as he realized she wasn't going to put up with any baloney from him—or any other man.

"Why pay for that when I'm prepared to analyze for free?" he said. Putting his head to the side, he pretended to study her. "Let's see if I've got a proper fix on you. You're headstrong, stubborn, sure you're usually right… and a hard worker."

His casual assumptions—as well as his cynical tone—were really annoying her, and she said the first thing that came to mind.

"So's your old man," she shot back.

His sudden grin was a stunner, white teeth flashing, eyes crinkling, and real humor lit up his face. "I didn't know you knew him."

Okay, there it was—the main thing she had to watch out for. Everything in her wanted to like him. He looked…well, nice. And that was even more dangerous than his undeniable sex appeal—the macho way he took charge so naturally; the breathtaking chest muscles that seemed to swell under his light polo shirt; the way he was poised, down on one knee before her, like a knight asking a lady for her scarf to wear into battle.

She blinked quickly and shook her head, furious at herself for letting her imagination run wild on that last one. What was she doing, sinking back into childhood? She'd spent a good part of her youth blocking out reality by creating a dream world in which she was a lost princess. She couldn't go back to that. Too much fantasy could corrupt her reasoning powers and that would be a gateway straight to the danger zone. She was a grown woman with a baby on the way and she couldn't indulge herself like this anymore. Life was tough—she had to be hard to survive it.

Still, that was difficult to do when the man she faced was so incredibly good-looking and dressed so well. Besides the blue polo shirt, he wore clean fashionable denim slacks that fit like a glove and a soft suede jacket that clung to him in all the right places. What a contrast to her slightly silly green waitress uniform. And also, what a clear picture of their different stations in life. He looked like he shopped at Neiman-Marcus. She looked like she hadn't shopped in years. Hardly princess material.

She looked away quickly, aware more than ever that they were alone. This was not a place she wanted to be. Besides, it was time she got back to work. Millie was shorthanded today and Annie didn't want to risk bad feelings at this job. She needed it badly, and there weren't many who would hire a woman almost seven months pregnant.

"May I go now?" she said, needing to ask as he was blocking her way.

He gazed at her levelly. "No, you may not. You're still pale and I don't like your pulse rate."

She flashed a quick glare his way. "There are things I don't like about you, but I've got the manners not to list them."

He made a comical face. "Impossible."

She frowned a little nervously. "What's impossible?"

"That there's something about me not to like." He

was grinning again. She really wished he wouldn't. "I'm a terrific guy. Everyone says so."

Great. That was all she needed. Not only was he incredibly handsome and a great dresser, he was popular, too. At least, if you asked him. Reaching up, she pushed her thick dark wavy hair back behind her ear.

"That's what happens when you depend on selective polling," she said coolly. Even if she looked like a waitress, she could act as snooty as any Dallas cattle heiress if she tried hard enough. "All the votes aren't in yet, mister."

One sleek dark eyebrow rose with just a touch of surprise. "Doctor," he corrected smoothly.

She blinked. "Doctor who?"

"No, that was the TV show. Just plain old Dr. Allman. Or better yet, Matt Allman."

She shook her head. Now he was being plain old annoying and he had to know it was bugging her. Was he doing it to put her down? Somehow she didn't really think so. It seemed more like teasing, like he thought he was being playful. Like he was attracted to her and—

No. Now that was going too far. Why would a man like this be attracted to a woman in ugly green who was carrying someone else's baby? That was just her fantasy side coming out again. She was going to have to learn to turn that little talent off.

"I should have known you were an Allman. I guess that explains it."

"Explains what?"

She flushed, not sure what to say. The Allmans had been one of the founding families of the town, but their reputation hadn't been good when she'd been here in the past. She always had the idea the Allmans were "this close" to being outlaws. Of course, that might have been pure gossip at the time, but something about the family always seemed to signal danger of one sort or another.

"That explains why you look as much like a rebel without a cause as you do a doctor," she said a bit lamely, knowing he was waiting for an answer.

"A rebel." He savored the word, eyes narrowing as though he saw himself from a distance. "I kind of like that."

"Of course you do. You're an Allman."

He thought for a moment, his penetrating gaze clearly taking stock of her. She stared right back at him, not giving an inch. But inside, she quivered, wondering what he saw. A mouthy waitress who ought to be more grateful for what he'd done to tend to her? A pain in the neck? A pitiful ragamuffin, her dark hair a tangled mess?

None of those things were good and she wished, suddenly, that she knew a way to act that wouldn't put her at odds with him. Sometimes it seemed she only had two speeds, mad attraction or complete hostility. And since she'd vowed she would never let herself get fooled by an attraction again, the tough-girl pose was just about all she had left.

But maybe that was okay. It gave her armor against falling for the sort of charm that had left her pregnant and alone. It helped let a man like this doctor know his handsome face and hunky physique weren't going to bowl her over any time soon. If she had to be hard and caustic to make that plain, so be it. Better he know right up front. Better they all know. And better that she keep in mind the consequences of letting silly romantic notions creep into her thinking.

"So I'm an Allman," he was saying, looking quizzical. "What exactly does that mean to you?"

She drew herself up a bit. "Do you really want to know?"

"Yes."

She sighed. "Okay. To me, growing up around here, the Allmans were cowboys, trending toward the wrong side of the law. The Allmans always seemed to be starting fights or causing trouble. Especially for the McLaughlins."

He laughed, and she flushed, not sure what he found so funny. He couldn't possibly know her relationship to the McLaughlins. No one knew. So that couldn't be it. Frowning, she went on.

"Now I come back to town and find the Allmans are the movers and shakers of the place. What happened?"

It was a remarkable transformation from what she'd seen. Those low-life Allmans now had a thriving company and the high-and-mighty McLaughlins had hit hard times. That had to be difficult for everyone concerned.

She'd been thirteen when her mother had finally told her that her father had been William McLaughlin, from the family she'd worked for years ago. And because that family was so important in Chivaree, she'd held the secret close and been proud of it. Watching McLaughlins whenever she came to town, she'd felt an identification with them that she couldn't communicate—and they had fascinated her.

Now, all alone with a baby coming, she'd come back instinctively to the place where her "family" lived, to find out a few things. First, was it true? Did she really have blood ties to these people? And second, would they accept her? Or would they want to deny that she had any right to their attention at all?

So far she hadn't decided exactly what she was going to do—which McLaughlin she would approach and what she would say when she did so. The man she'd been told was her father had died a few years before, so that bit of closure would be forever denied to her. But he'd had other children, three sons. What would they say when she showed up on their doorsteps?

Soon after she'd arrived in town, she'd found a way to insert herself into the McLaughlin consciousness. She'd seen a wanted notice for a once-a-week housekeeper at the McLaughlin Ranch, and she'd applied for the job right away. Since she was only working part-time here at Millie's, she had plenty of time for it, and the housekeeping job gave her a sort of foot in the door. The fact that she was working in a position very like what her mother had once had with the family was a little troubling. But she couldn't be choosy at this point. She needed to get the lay of the land. Time was moving on and a baby was coming. And she knew she was going to have to do something about that very soon.

"What's your name?" he was asking.

"Annie Torres." The first name was pinned to her uniform, but she wondered if he would recognize the last name. Probably not. After all, why would he remember the name of the McLaughlin housekeeper from so many years ago? The McLaughlins themselves hadn't.

"Nice to meet you, Annie," he said casually. "In time I hope you'll come to see that Allmans aren't so bad."

"But that doesn't mean you're now the good guys," she said hastily. "Just because you're rich and all."

"Oh? Why not?"

She shrugged, turning her palms up. "Leopards and zebras."

He looked as though he wasn't sure he'd heard correctly. "What?"

"Spots and stripes don't change that easily."

"Ah." He nodded wisely. "Wolves in sheep's clothing."

"Exactly right." She gave him a skeptical look. "For all we know, you could be playing possum."

He groaned. "Are you always this glib with the animal aphorisms?"

A small spark of satisfaction flared in her chest. She finally felt as though one of her barbs had hit home. "Not always. I'm as game for a good sports metaphor as the next girl."

"Good." He rose and held out a hand to her. "Because you're being traded."

"What?" For some reason, maybe because she was still trying to figure out what he was talking about, she meekly let him take her hand and pull her to her feet.

"How do you feel?" he asked, studying her eyes.

She took a deep breath. He hadn't let go of her hand, but maybe that was to help her steady herself. Frowning, she pulled her hand out of his and rubbed it against her skirt, trying to erase the delicious feeling his touch had given her.

"I'm fine," she said crisply. "I need to get back to work."

He shook his head. "Negative. I'm taking you in to my clinic. You need a thorough checkup."

"I *need* not to lose my job," she told him, trying to maneuver around him toward the door and failing to make any headway.

"You're quitting this job," he told her, looking intently into her eyes for a moment. "Doctor's orders."

This was crazy. It was all very well to tell her not to work too hard, to get plenty of rest and keep her feet up and so forth. But the fact remained that she had to make a living somehow. Lifting her chin, she glared at him defiantly.

"Doctors can throw their weight around all they want, but patients have still got to eat."

She turned toward the door but he moved to block her progress and she looked up, a little startled by how big he was, how wide his shoulders seemed. And how knowing his gaze seemed to be. Did this man ever have any doubts about anything?

"You'll eat," he said. "I've got another job for you. One that won't keep you on your feet all day."

She wondered why he so casually assumed she would trust him enough to hand over life's little decisions to him.

"And that would be…?"

"Office work. My office assistant abandoned me. She's gone back East to help her fiancé pass the New York state bar exam. I need someone to fill in until she gets back."

Office work. Air-conditioning. A soft, plush seat. Regular hours. It sounded heavenly. But it never paid as much as waiting tables and getting tips.

"How long will that be?" she asked anyway, tempted against her better judgment.

"At least three months." His grin had become endearingly crooked. "That fiancé of hers needs a lot of work and she's the determined type."

She looked at him curiously. "What makes you think I'd be good at doing the sort of office work you need done?"

He shrugged. "I've seen you working here with Millie over the last few weeks. Competence just radiates from you. Don't you know that?"

It was a nice compliment, but she hesitated, then shook her head.

"I can't quit here," she said, putting a hand on her rounded belly. "I'm totally dependent on what I make and I need to save for my recovery period after the baby comes."

His blue eyes darkened. "No husband handy?"

He asked it quietly, no moral judgment implied, and she felt a small twinge of gratitude for that. She'd spent too much emotional energy lately in resenting the looks and comments made by people once they realized her situation. No one could be more contemptuous of her idiocy in landing in this fix than she was. She didn't need to hear it from others. Lifting her head, she met his gaze with a steady look.

"No. I'm not married."

If anything, his gaze grew warmer. "No family of any sort?"

She shook her head. "My mother died about a year ago."

"And your father?"

"I don't have one."

He frowned. "Everyone has a father."

"Only in the biological sense," she said.

She could tell he didn't like that answer, but he let it go.

"How much do you make?"

She told him. It wasn't like it was a secret. Everyone knew how much this job took in. She didn't add the amount she made at her second job, but he didn't need to know that.

"You'll do better working for me." He told her a figure that got her attention. "And you'll get benefits, too. You'll need that for when you have the baby."

She shook her head. "My delivery fees will be covered." She hesitated only a second or two, then went on. "I'm considering giving my baby up for adoption. The lawyer will take care of everything."

The very air seemed to go still. And at the same time, something flashed across his face. He looked as though her statement had stunned him. His face was like stone but his eyes were blazing.

"What?" he said softly.

She licked her dry lips. She had expected surprise, maybe bemusement, but nothing like this.

"I think you heard me. Why the shock and amazement? I'm not married."

She hated having to explain. The pain of having to make this decision bled freshly every time. She threw up her hands, half a gesture of exasperation, half a plea for understanding.

"I want what's best for my baby. Adoption can be a

wonderful thing. A nice couple who can't have a child of their own would be a lot better for this child than anything I can promise."

She hated that she sounded defensive, but there it was.

The muscle at his jaw worked for a moment as his gaze seemed to cut through to her bones. Was it the fact that she was considering putting her baby up for adoption that was bothering him so much? She didn't know what else it could be. Something was sure going on inside him. Some emotional chord had been yanked with a vengeance. She watched curiously, wondering what he was thinking as his gaze dropped to study her rounded belly. But his eyes were cool and impenetrable and his face was giving nothing away.

"Let's go," he said shortly, putting a hand in the center of her back to help lead her out the door.

She balked. That hand felt too good—and too controlling at the same time. "Wait a minute. I'm feeling a bit bulldozed here."

He nodded. "You want some time to think it over?"

"Yes. That would be helpful."

His smile was humorless. "You'll have plenty of time in the car on the way to the clinic."

"But—"

"Am I going to have to pick you up and carry you again?"

She drew in her breath sharply. "No." Biting her lip, she let him lead her. After all, what choice did she have?

Chapter Two

"I hope you don't think I'm taking any clothes off."

The first thing Annie noticed when she and Matt arrived at the clinic was that the place was empty. It was getting late. Obviously, the staff had all gone home for the night. Still, it made her feel a bit awkward. Not to mention suspicious.

That was actually somewhat new for her, but she was learning. *Don't trust anyone, especially studly-looking men with flattering words and a roving eye.* She tugged her light sweater tightly around her shoulders and glared at Matt as though he were the archetypal representative of that very group.

"Because any test that needs me naked isn't going to happen," she added, just for emphasis.

To her surprise, instead of getting annoyed, he laughed out loud as he turned to look at her.

"No need for to strip down for this," he assured her.

Ushering her into the room where various types of medical examination machines stood around like alert soldiers, he glanced at the way she was hugging her clothes around herself.

"But tell me—do you usually bundle up as though expecting snow when you're preparing to be examined by a doctor?"

"Not with my *real* doctor," she said archly.

"What do you think I am?" he asked as he motioned for her to take a seat on the end of the table. "A phony doctor?"

"That remains to be seen."

Sliding the blood pressure cuff up her arm, he gave her a sardonic look. "So who is your *real* doctor?" he asked.

"Dr. Marin."

He nodded, adjusting the tester and inflating the cuff, then listening as he watched it count down.

"Ah yes, Raul Marin," he said as he released her again. "His son was a friend of mine in high school." He jotted down her blood pressure reading and turned to get the fetal monitor set up. "Well, if you prefer, I can take you over to his office. It's after office hours, but—"

"But that's just the point. I don't need a doctor. I need to go home."

She frowned. How had she let him talk her into coming here, anyway? What she said was true. She needed to go home, get into bed, pull the covers up…and wait for all this to end.

But her argument didn't seem to be swaying him at all.

"I think we can get a few tests in right now. Enough to reassure me that you and this baby are doing okay."

"Oh, well, as long as *you're* reassured, the world can rest easy tonight."

Her sarcasm fell on deaf ears. He jotted down some figures on a chart, then turned and motioned for her to lie back on the table.

"Let's see how that little guy is," he said.

"Little guy." She liked that. She'd purposefully avoided finding out the gender of her baby, and resisted the temptation to name the child. If she was going to give the baby up for adoption, becoming too close and intimate would just make things that much harder. But when he said "little guy," her heart skipped a beat and she felt a sudden surge of warmth that almost brought tears to her eyes. He was obviously ready to feel an easy affection for this new life she was carrying. She had to blink hard to keep from letting him see how that touched her.

"Okay, Doctor."

He glanced into her eyes. "Call me Matt."

She bit her lip. "How about Mr. Allman?"

A muscle twitched at his jaw. She was finally needling him just a little too much, and when he responded, there was a thread of annoyance in his tone.

"Whatever, Annie. Call me Dumbo if that makes you feel safer." He moved closer, freeing some cords that had become tangled. "Now just relax and we'll get this over with."

She put a hand over her belly, automatically protective. The baby was doing just fine. She was sure of it—as sure as she could be. She was taking all the right vitamins and appearing regularly for her checkups, even though it was difficult to pay for them. She might be seriously considering giving her baby up to someone else to raise, but that was because of how much she loved him…or her. She'd never felt so close to anything in her life as she felt to this baby.

"How much do you charge?" she asked warily as she watched him prepare the monitor. She had some money saved and she didn't want him to think she was expecting a handout.

He waved the question away. "First exams are freebies."

For some reason, that irritated her. She wasn't a charity case. She could pay her own way, even if it was hard sometimes.

"If you're giving people freebies all over the place," she said crisply, "I don't see how you're going to make enough to keep any sort of staff for long."

He looked up after strapping her up to the monitor and laughed aloud. "My God, I'm hiring someone who actually understands how things work. Keep this up and I'll have to make you office manager."

It was humiliating how those half-mocking words of praise made her glow with satisfaction. She had to cover that up quickly.

"You can't *make* me into anything."

He didn't bother to respond. He'd caught on long ago to the fact that most of her words didn't mean a thing and were just a way to keep him at arm's length. That was okay. Although he understood her need to protect herself, he just wanted to make sure that she didn't lose sight of what was important—the welfare of this baby she was carrying.

He'd noticed her over the last few weeks, whenever he'd stopped by Millie's for a quick bite. He'd been keeping an eye on the evidence of her baby's progress, though he'd never said anything to her until she'd dropped into a faint at his feet. She had a bright, intelligent look to her that he'd liked and he'd wondered about her. He'd noticed that there was no wedding ring and it reminded him of his own unsettling situation….

It had only been a few weeks since an old friend passing through the area had called and innocently asked him what had ever happened to Penny Hagar, a young woman Matt had dated in Dallas a couple of years before. And then he'd asked about the baby.

"Baby?" Matt had responded, startled. "What baby?"

That was the first hint he'd ever had that Penny had become pregnant during their relationship. Since that day, searching for Penny and her baby had begun to consume more and more of his time and energy. He'd hired a private investigator once his own efforts had come up dry. So far, even the professional wasn't having any luck. But the whole affair had made him much more aware of the babies around him. The world seemed to be full of them. Including the one Annie was carrying. And considering giving away.

"So what kind of staff do you have, anyway?" Annie asked, assuming she would be working right alongside them soon.

"Here in this office? There are two of us family practice physicians. We've got a combination receptionist-bookkeeper, a practical nurse and an RN. We're thinking of hiring a physician's assistant, too."

She blinked, taking all that in. "So where exactly will I fit in?"

Turning, he looked at her. "I guess I didn't make myself clear. You won't be working here. I've also got an office at Allman Industries. That's where I'm going to need you."

"Allman Industries." She said the words slowly, thinking it over. There had been no such thing as Allman Industries when she'd lived here off and on as a child, but she'd heard it mentioned since she'd come back. As she remembered, it was housed in a big old building just off Main Street, one of those structures with gargoyles at the corners, looking like something that came from times gone by.

"Does that meet with your approval?" he asked her, getting a little sarcastic himself.

"I don't know," she said pertly. "We'll have to see."

He nodded. "I'll be awaiting your judgment with bated breath," he said. "What I need at the office is someone to keep track of what the hell I'm doing. I'm basically the company medical staff at Allman's, but I keep getting drafted into business meetings as well. My father is doing his best to lure me away from medicine. What he'd really like is for me to take over the company. It gets a little difficult to know where I am or what I'm supposed to be doing sometimes."

She couldn't imagine him having trouble telling anyone what he wanted or what he thought they should be doing. The man exuded confidence.

"Why don't you just tell him you don't have time for the meetings?"

He stared at her for a long moment before responding. Then he grinned. "Why indeed? That will be your first assignment. Tell everyone who calls that I'm too busy to accommodate them. You don't know how that would simplify my life."

She shrugged. "That seems easy enough."

A series of expressions moved across his face. She didn't know if he was amused or incredulous.

"You just wait," he said, shaking his head and laughing softly.

"And I can assist you with some of the medical stuff, too," she said, suddenly feeling she needed to explain that she had certain skills that deserved recognition.

"I don't think so," he said. "You don't have any nursing training."

"But I do."

That got his attention. He straightened and stared at her. "What?"

"I was in my second year at Houston Medical School in the nursing program when I got pregnant and had to drop out."

He made a whistling sound. "Wow. That will be very helpful."

She shrugged. "I don't have certification."

"No. And of course, you won't be expected to take over any nursing duties. But just to know you're experienced will be a big help. In a town like this, every little bit of knowledge counts."

He favored her with a lopsided grin that hinted at a new respect for her. That curled her toes for some unknown reason.

"So you see, you were always meant for this job," he said. "Kismet."

Kismet. She shivered. She knew the word just meant *fate,* but she didn't like it. There was something romantic about it and romance was something she was dead set against.

And that reminded her of something. Millie's beautiful daughter Shelley was set to marry Matt's brother Rafe. Everyone at the café had been buzzing about nothing else for days. Annie liked Shelley a lot, and she'd been just as interested as anyone in the progress toward the ceremony. Now she wondered about Matt. She knew he wasn't married, but she couldn't help but speculate about why that was. He was successful and attractive and wasn't getting any younger. Men like him were usually spoken for by now.

"Okay, Doc," she said, forcing a stern frown. Craning her neck, she looked at the monitor screen. "What's the verdict?"

"You and the baby seem fine."

The sense of relief she felt surprised her. She hadn't realized she might be more than a little concerned.

"You see? All that worrying for nothing."

"No." He shook his head. "It's never for nothing."

He had that one right. The longer she hung around this man, the more attractive he was looking. Reason enough to worry. Reason enough to be very, very careful.

And time to escape from this situation.

"You going to let me out of this thing?" she asked.

"Sure. Hold on."

He was turning off switches on the fetal monitor and

she watched, starting to feel pretty darn pleased with herself. She'd been in close proximity to this very appealing man—he'd even had his hands on various parts of her body and had leaned very close a few times, so close that she could feel his body heat and catch a hint of some sort of clean and soapy scent—and had been assaulted with all sorts of tempting male virility. Yet she'd remained completely unmoved by it. She was doing okay. She wasn't even hyperventilating.

Hooray for me, she thought silently, giving herself a little smile.

And then, as he removed the strap, his hand brushed her breast. She froze and her gaze jerked up to meet his. Intentions were everything and she needed to see his, right now. What she saw didn't make her feel any better.

There was no hint of any intention to mess with her, or even to take the chance at a little touching. But there was something else that was even worse. Something in his eyes held hers for a beat too long and while it did, she felt a jolt, a sudden connection, a new sensual awareness that snapped between them and made her gasp.

His eyes changed. He knew exactly what she was thinking.

"Sorry," he murmured, turning to put away the equipment.

But she was breathless and desperate not to let him know, slowly pulling air into her lungs and forcing back the panicky feeling in her chest.

"If you want to get your things together, I'll drive you home," he said, still working with the equipment.

If only it was that easy. If only she could zing back

a one-liner that would singe his hair. If only she could tell him to take a hike, that she could just darn well take care of that herself. But she didn't have her car and she didn't have any friends she could call. So unless she wanted to walk across town as night set in, she would have to let Matt drive her home.

She closed her eyes for a moment, making a silent promise. As soon as she could, she was going to get out of this mess. And once she was back on her feet, she was never, ever going to put herself in this kind of dependency again. One way or another, she was going to take control of her life.

Cruising slowly down the side street and turning on Main, Matt glanced at Annie. Somehow she managed to look as if she were perched on the edge of her seat despite the seat belt that had her securely strapped in. A casual observer would have thought she was being abducted. She looked ready to wrench the door handle open and leap from the car once she got the chance.

Shaking his head, he stifled the impulse to let her know how annoying it was to be treated as if he were conducting a shanghaiing operation. But he was pretty sure complaining would only make things worse. He couldn't yell at someone to stop being so scared of everything. That didn't ever work.

He wasn't sure how he'd ended up taking care of her anyway. He was too busy for this. He'd only gone into Millie's to grab piece of pie and a cup of coffee that was supposed to keep him awake while he worked late at his office at Allman Industries, and the next thing he knew, he was volunteering to take charge of another stray being.

That was what she reminded him of: an injured animal. As a boy he'd been famous for bringing home lost things—puppies, kittens, a garter snake, a baby skunk. He remembered a wounded bird he'd once found. He'd carried the poor thing around in a shoe box, doing everything a ten-year-old kid could think of to help it heal. He'd lavished all sorts of attention on it, trying to get it to eat and drink, and it had learned to stay still in his hands. But the look in its bright black eyes was always wary, as though it was sure, despite all his kindness, that he was probably going to hurt it in the end. And that was the look he saw in her eyes as well.

He felt a quick stab of anger at whoever had done this to her. A woman just didn't get this skittish without cause. He wanted to soothe her, tell her not to worry, but he knew that anything he said might just make things worse.

"So tell me, what made you head back to Chivaree?" he asked, hoping he sounded casual.

She glanced at him sideways. "I told you. I lived here when I was a kid."

"Did you go to Chivaree schools?"

"Off and on."

This was like pulling teeth. She'd dropped the smart-aleck attitude, but now she was being so stingy with her answers, he almost wished she'd come back with another good insult.

"How about your baby. Boy or girl?" he asked.

"I don't know. I haven't asked."

He looked over at her, puzzled. "You don't want to know?"

"I'll know soon enough."

He grimaced, his eyes back on the road. "You're keeping your distance, aren't you? Trying not to get attached."

She turned away. She wasn't going to get into this with him, especially knowing how he felt about it.

"How about you?" she asked instead. "Have any children?"

He didn't answer right away and she looked at him, surprised.

"I've never been married," he said at last.

She shrugged. "Neither have I."

Turning the car off Main Street, he headed toward the side of town she'd told him to aim for. Chivaree had changed a lot over the last few years. Used to be the place had a lonely, wind-swept look that wouldn't have seemed out of place in an old-fashioned Western. But lately the population had surged and new subdivisions were going up on the hills around the town. Chain stores and restaurants were opening up near the highway. Growth was good but it carried with it the inevitable costs.

"Turn left at the next stop sign," she told him.

He nodded, then frowned as he made the turn. He didn't much like the look of the neighborhood. He hadn't been on this seedy side of town for a while. Things had gotten worse in this crime-infested area.

"You living with somebody?" he asked hopefully. He didn't want to face the possibility that she hung around here alone.

"No."

"You're all on your own?"

"Yes."

"You should have someone else with you."

She gave him what sounded almost like a snort. "That's a nice theory. But the fact is, I don't have anybody. I'm fine on my own."

Fine on her own, huh? Then why did she sound so defensive?

She glanced at him sideways. He couldn't help admiring that flash of her dark eyes and the way her thick, chocolate-colored hair swirled around her face.

"Here it is. Pull over behind that red car."

He pulled over and turned off the engine, grimacing as he looked at the grungy building she had indicated.

"Thanks for everything," she said with a breezy tone he knew she was forcing. "I'll see you at Allman Industries in the morning."

"Wait a second. I'll walk you to the door."

She flinched as though that startled her.

"No," she said quickly, that wary look on her pretty face again. "Don't."

He frowned at her. "Why not?"

She ran her tongue across her lower lip nervously. "The neighbors will see you."

"The neighbors?" He stared at her incredulously. "So what?"

"They'll talk."

"They'll talk? Just because I act like a gentleman and—"

"They don't know from gentlemen around here." She pulled her things together and released her seat belt, ready to fly. "The men they see around here are no gentlemen."

His eyes narrowed. "Are you telling me—?"

She glanced at him. "Yes. They'll think—" She shrugged and looked away. "Just let me go alone. I don't need to be fodder for gossip."

He bit down on his tongue. Anger was threatening to take over if he didn't smother it fast. Taking a deep breath, he turned and challenged her.

"Annie, what the hell are you doing living in this kind of neighborhood?"

She lifted her chin defiantly. "The rent's cheap."

"Sometimes cheap is the most expensive of all."

"Listen, Matt. I don't come from money. I was raised by a single mother who did what she could, but couldn't do much. I've lived in places like this lots of times in my life. I can handle it."

Giving him a reassuring look, she slipped out of the car and walked quickly toward the entrance to her building.

He sat where he was, staring after her. He didn't like it. This was no kind of neighborhood to bring a newborn baby back to. He shrugged away the fact that she was considering putting her baby up for adoption.

Assuming, for the sake of this argument, she would be bringing a baby home from the hospital, how was she going to cope in a place like this?

Well, maybe she had some friends.

No. She'd only been in town a month, so she couldn't possibly have built up the sort of friendships that went with providing for a baby's needs.

He thought of her, of her pretty face and those dark,

beautiful eyes. She didn't belong here. He wanted to throw caution to the wind and stomp in after her, grab her and—

Yeah, then what? He didn't know anything about housing here in Chivaree. For all he knew, she was right and this was all that was available. On the other hand, once he got her installed at his office in the Allman building, once he started paying her a decent wage, maybe she would be able to afford a better place. He knew that was a better course. If he tried to go in and force her into doing things the way he thought they should be done, he was going to put her back up permanently.

He almost grinned, thinking of how fierce her pretty face would get, how her perfect little chin would jut out as she defied him. She was a charmer in her own way. Funny how hard she tried to resist that.

Still, the more he thought about it, the more he knew this was just an unacceptable place for her to live. No employee of his should live like this.

He grimaced. Who was he trying to kid? Annie wasn't going to be just any employee. That baby she was carrying was taking on larger than life proportions in his mind—and it was no mystery to him why that was.

It had only been a few weeks since he'd found out he had a child himself. Out there in the world somewhere was a baby he'd never known about. That was a completely mind-blowing concept and he still wasn't used to it. So many questions remained unanswered.

It made him sick to think that Penny, the ex-girlfriend who'd had his child and never told him, might have had to live in places like this dump where Annie was staying. But from what he'd learned so far, she'd been on her own when she was getting ready to go through delivery…and preparing to put the baby up for adoption, just as Annie was thinking of doing. So chances were, she'd had to take what she could get at the time.

It was hard thinking that while he was casually going on with his life, laughing, dating, getting a residency in family practice in Dallas, Penny had been taking on all the responsibilities he should have been sharing with her. And that she had made the solo decision to give up her baby—*his baby*—to someone else.

He should have been there.

Maybe he thought helping Annie would make amends to a certain degree. Could that be part of his interest in Annie and what was to become of her? Sure, he knew it was nuts to get involved. And maybe he *was* crazy. But babies had to be protected. Absolutely. A no-brainer. And if he had to take on the mantle of guardian angel, he would.

He switched the engine on and started slowly down the street, but his mind was still back at the grungy apartment building with Annie.

Chapter Three

Annie's eyes shot open. She stared into the dark, wondering what had jolted her awake this way. Had it been a scream? A gunshot? She'd heard plenty of both those things since she'd moved into this dank, dark room.

There was a thump and someone began yelling in the hallway. She tried to relax. *Them* again. It was just the couple next door. The woman was always throwing her partner's things out the window and then he would storm up the stairs, yelling and pounding on the door she'd locked against him. The yelling would go on, back and forth, for what seemed like hours. Finally she would let him back in the apartment and then dishes would crash into walls and he would yell and she would scream. The ridiculous thing was, once they made up, the lovemaking was just as noisy as the fighting had been.

Meanwhile, the people in the apartment on the other

side of her had turned on some strange foreign music, very loud. She knew they were doing it to drown out the fighting, but it was almost worse. Pulling her pillow up over her head she groaned. How was she going to start a new job in the morning with no sleep at all?

Something hit the wall hard and she jerked in response, adrenaline surging. This was impossible. But more than that, it was scary. One of these days she had a feeling something worse than her peace being disturbed would happen. Matt had been right. She had to find another place to live. But how? With no money beyond just enough to feed herself and pay for this place, life was tough.

The woman screamed again and Annie winced. This was just too awful. And the worst was not knowing whether she should call the police again or not. Was the screaming for real? Or just a weapon the woman used against her boyfriend? Annie didn't know how much more of this she could stand.

Suddenly there was a new voice and she raised her head, listening intently. The yelling was more hysterical and the thumps sounded more like a real fight. And then, there was nothing. Silence.

She sat up, frowning. What the heck was going on? The fights were never over this quickly.

Someone banged on her door. She jumped a foot into the air and cried out softly.

Her heart was thumping so hard it felt like it might burst. She closed her eyes for half a second to catch herself, then slipped from the bed and ran softly to the door, just listening, trying to figure out what kind of monster might be on the other side. Was it the man who had been yelling? The woman looking for refuge? The new voice she'd heard?

"Annie? Are you in there? Are you okay?"

It took her a moment to realize it was Matt Allman, and once she did, joy burst inside her.

"Matt?" She tugged on the multiple locks, sliding each back in turn and opening the door. "What are you doing here?"

He looked very good standing there—all tall and dark and strong and male. Just what she needed right now. Relief swept through her and she did something completely unexpected and totally ridiculous. She threw herself into his arms.

It only lasted for seconds, and she jumped back away from him again so quickly, he might have thought he'd imagined the whole thing. But for those few seconds, his warm arms had felt so good against her almost-naked body, her head was spinning.

"Where did you come from?" she asked, backing into her apartment again. A strange fuzzy place in her sleepy mind seemed to think he might have appeared in a puff of smoke. But the strong, protective arms around her had been so real, she might never get that short but sweet memory out of her head.

"I came to get you," he responded calmly. "Get your things together. Let's go."

She stared at him blankly. "I—I can't go. It's after midnight," she added irrationally.

"It'll only get later the longer you procrastinate," he told her gruffly. He glanced down the hall, then looked back at her, his gaze taking in the lacy nightgown and her slender body showing through it. "Let me in. I'll help you get your things ready to go."

She knew she was probably crazy for letting him into her lonely apartment in the middle of the night. After all, the way he'd looked at her had reminded her of just how nearly transparent her nightgown was in the light from the hallway. Not good. Even a pregnant woman might look enticing in flimsy lace in the middle of the night.

"Oh," she said, looking down. Maybe she could ask him to wait in the hall until—

But he wasn't waiting any longer. And suddenly there he was, inside her apartment, closing her door.

"Come on. I'm getting you out of here."

She shook her head, then glanced around for her robe. "No. Where would I go?" she said, lifting it off a chair and slipping it on, hugging it close to her chest. "This is where I live, I—"

He grabbed her arm. She looked up at him, startled. He obviously meant business.

"Look, if you want me to get all caveman on you, I will. Bottom line, I'm not going to let you sleep here one more night."

"But—"

"Annie, be reasonable. It was like World War Three in your hallway when I got here. I had to kick some butt to get them to quiet down. There's no way you can live with this stuff going on." He glared at her. "Don't you ever call the cops on these people?"

She nodded. "I've tried that. They came once, but they don't like to come over here to this neighborhood."

He groaned. "Annie, I mean it. You're coming with me. You have no other option."

Looking in his eyes, she knew there was no point arguing. Turning, she looked at her closet. "Okay. Let me change and—"

"No time for that. Grab your toothbrush and let's get out of here. We can get the rest of your things tomorrow."

Matt took charge. In no time at all she was sitting in the passenger seat of his car, cruising through the dark streets. She was wearing her robe over her nightgown, but her hair was billowing wildly around her head and her feet were in thongs. She did have her toothbrush clutched firmly in her hand. At least there was that.

"I don't know why I'm letting you do this," she said, shaking her head at her own folly.

He glanced at her and a half smile softened the hard edges of his face. "I don't know why either. But it's probably because you know I'm right."

She sighed. "I'll bet you're right a lot of the time, aren't you?" she said.

He shrugged. "Pretty much all the time if you want to know the truth."

She was quiet for a moment, thinking about what might be coming next. She supposed he was taking her back to his place. Where else was he going to take her in the middle of the night? She had to be out of her mind for going along with this. After all, she might have to listen to fights at her place, but at least she was just a spectator, so far. At Matt's apartment she would probably be one of the main combatants. Because if he thought her gratitude for his concern was going to get him anything, he could think again!

She bristled, ready to hate him. Men were all alike, weren't they? A pregnant woman with no man around seemed to act like catnip on the average male. She'd better get ready to let him know just what she thought of lechers. Bracing herself, she waited for him to turn down the street where all the new apartment buildings stood.

But he didn't turn there. He just kept going and she looked at him in surprise.

"Where are you taking me?" she asked.

"Home," he said shortly, not taking his gaze off the road.

She frowned, looking out at the simple frame houses they were passing.

"Whose home?" she countered.

"We're here," Matt said instead of answering her question. He pulled the car up a driveway to stop in front of a house that had obviously once been just like all the other simple frame houses on the block, but had since morphed into something much more grandiose.

"The Allman homestead," he said, squinting as he looked through the windshield at it.

She leaned forward to stare at it, too. The place looked huge, three stories tall, with gables and a round tower, as though someone had taken a liking to the Queen Anne style somewhere along the way. To Annie it looked like a fairy-tale house, with windows for princesses to lean out of and dark recesses for villains to hide in.

"The reason it looks sort of odd is that Pop keeps putting on additions," Matt said. "If he had his way, every Allman would marry and keep his family right here, so there's got to be plenty of room."

"That seems very..." She was about to say *generous,* but she had second thoughts. *Controlling* was probably a better word. "Wait a minute. You live here with your family?"

"Sure."

She looked at the house with alarm. "Are you going to tell me this place is full of Allmans of all shapes and sizes?"

"Yup."

She swallowed hard. She was a McLaughlin, even if he didn't know it. The Allmans and the McLaughlins were like the Hatfields and the McCoys. They didn't mix, didn't speak, didn't tolerate each other at all. And here she was being ushered into the belly of the beast. Yikes! Was this really a good idea?

She was stalling for time and he made an impatient gesture.

"Come on, Annie," he said, sliding out of the driver's seat and coming around to help her out. "Keep it kind of quiet, though. Everyone's in bed."

"So who all's here right now?" she asked, looking nervously up at the second-floor windows.

"Let's see." Leading her across the lawn, he started counting on his fingers. "Pop, two sisters, Rita and Jodie, my brother David...and me."

She came to a dead stop, horrified, as the magnitude of it all rose up in front of her. "I can't go in there."

He frowned at her. "Why not?"

"Because…what is your family going to think?"

He groaned. "You care too much what other people think. Don't worry about them. I'll explain it all to them in the morning." She still didn't move and he added, "Look, where else are you going to go?"

Well, that was it, wasn't it? She had no choice. How the heck had she let this happen to her again? He was right. She looked at him, feeling frustrated and a bit angry. She hated being in this position. But she knew she was going to have to give in to the inevitable. Unless she wanted to sleep in the car.

"Listen, don't worry about it," he said, still trying to convince her. "We've got a lot of extra rooms."

She blinked. "There will be a room just for me?" she asked incredulously.

"Sure."

Touching his arm, she looked up at him searchingly. "So—let me get this straight. You're not trying to smuggle me into your bedroom?"

He opened his mouth to say something, closed it again, then half laughed. "Annie-girl," he said in his best Texas drawl, "you're nervous as a cat in a dog pound. Don't you ever drop the suspicions? You'd think you'd never met a stranger who didn't turn out to be a horse thief."

She shrugged. "The good ones are rare as hen's teeth," she muttered, turning to look at the house again. "But I've still got hopes for you."

He grinned. "You and me both." He tugged on her arm to make her face him and looked down earnestly.

"Annie, I'm interested in two things. Number one, getting a good employee. And number two, making sure your baby is okay. Got that?"

"My baby is fine," she said, knowing the words sounded defensive. Again.

"Good," he said. "Let's keep it that way."

She stood where she was, frowning at him. His handsome face was contorted by the harsh light from the porch, but his determination was clear. This was something more than his professionalism as a physician.

She didn't get it. And because she didn't get it, she was suspicious. What was his angle, anyway?

"You do understand that I'm probably putting this baby up for adoption," she reminded him.

A flash of something that looked close to pain came and went across his face so quickly, she wasn't sure if she'd imagined it.

"So you say."

She shook her head, trying to puzzle him out and failing at it. "Why does this bother you so much?"

"Who said it bothered me?" He started to turn away, then slowly turned back as though he'd thought better of it. "It's just that…well, I want to make sure you think this through."

She fought back a wave of weariness. Did he really think she'd come up with this idea on the fly? It had been the hardest, most heart-breaking dilemma she'd ever faced. How could it be anything else?

"Believe me, I've done plenty of thinking about it."

"A lot of people don't. A lot of people just let things happen without looking ahead to the consequences."

He stared at her as though he expected her to take his words to heart—and maybe do something as a result. "And later, they regret it."

She was tempted to resent his words, but she had a sudden insight that changed her attitude. He was regretting something himself, she could tell. It was written all over him.

She couldn't ask him what it was. They just didn't know each other well enough for that. But she could ask him to explain something else she'd been wondering about.

"Matt," she said, studying his face. "What made you come over to my place tonight the way you did? Were you planning to get me to leave with you even before you saw what was going on in the hallway?"

"Sure," he said candidly, his eyes dark as night in the midnight-blue shadows. "I couldn't sleep thinking about you and that baby staying in that hellhole."

She drew herself up. "So you came on over to manage my life for me?"

Exasperation filled his face.

"Annie, you can go ahead and be outraged if you want to. I don't care. I only did what I had to do. Sue me." And he turned on his heel, striding toward the porch steps.

"I just might," she muttered, coming behind him, clutching her robe in close. It was a weak threat at best. And she really wasn't outraged, or even angry.

In fact, deep inside, she felt a warm sense of relief in having someone to lean on, even if for a very short period of time. Being pregnant and alone was the pits. And now, for better or for worse, she had a friend. Even if he was an Allman.

They moved quietly through the darkened house and up the wide stairway. Matt led her down a long hallway, then stopped and pushed open a door.

"Here you go."

He held the door open and she looked inside. The room was small but nicely furnished with a dresser sporting a huge mirror, a small desk with a chair, and a storybook bed with a fluffy canopy.

"Oh," she said, alarmed. This was too nice. "Are you sure this isn't somebody's room?"

"It's yours for the time being," he said. "But you're going to have to share the bathroom." He gestured toward it. "Girls' is on the south end of the hall, guys' on the north."

She wasn't even listening. She was still turning slowly, enchanted by the room. There was a framed sampler on one wall, a turn-of-the-century picture of farm life on another. The curtains and the bedspread matched the canopy. It was the sort of room she'd dreamed of having when she was a teenager, especially during those awful periods when she and her mother had been living in their car when they couldn't find a relative to stay with.

"Wow," she said, shaking her head. "Do I really deserve all this?"

He frowned, watching her pleasure in the room and not sure why it disturbed him. But it did.

But then, a lot about her disturbed him—like the way her body had felt against his when she'd leaped into his arms at her apartment. Like the way her breasts looked when the robe fell open. Like the way her dark eyes seemed to see into his soul in a way that made him wonder if his secrets were hidden well enough.

"What does *deserving* have to do with anything?" he said gruffly. "This is what's available. That's all."

"That's all," she echoed, spinning around and ending up right in front of him. "This is so great. Thank you, Matt!" And, seized with impulsive gratitude, she threw her arms around his neck and kissed his cheek.

Startled, he turned toward her. They jostled. Her body was there again, so soft and firm at the same time, sending his senses out the window and his judgment around the bend. Then his mouth found her lips and he realized it was pointless to fight the inevitable—a kiss was going to happen no matter what.

There was no doubt he'd been thinking about her. He couldn't get her off his mind. She'd filled every thought he'd had since he'd seen her crumple to the floor of Millie's. She'd been the reason he'd sprawled on his bed and stared at the ceiling for two hours before he finally decided to get up and do something about it. But he thought he'd been thinking about her as a very pretty, very attractive baby transportation device. It had all been about the baby in his mind.

Or maybe not. It seemed there was something else going on, some dark, urgent undercurrent he'd been trying to ignore. But it was there. And now he knew.

The taste of her soft mouth as it yielded to his, the feel of her high, firm breasts against his chest, the fresh scent of her skin, was all so good, so intoxicating—and arousing.

Oh, hell. He was getting turned on by a pregnant woman. What was he, crazy?

He pulled back at the same time she did, but if his reaction was regret, hers was outrage.

"Omigod, I should have known better!" Hands balled into fists and eyebrows knit together in anger, she looked around for her toothbrush. "I'm getting out of here."

"No, no." He grabbed her by the shoulders and forced her to look into his face. "Look Annie, I don't know how that happened. That just got away from me. Really. It's late and I'm tired and…" He shrugged, knowing his excuses were lame ones. "That's the sort of thing I never do. Never."

After she'd calmed a bit, he felt secure in releasing her shoulders. And when he did, she stood still instead of bolting.

"You'll be safe. You can stay here. Look there's a lock on the inside of the door. You can just lock yourself in and never come out. I can't get to you without an ax."

"You swear?" She searched his eyes uncertainly. "Because I didn't come here with you for this."

He groaned. "I know that. I didn't mean to do it. You're just—" He shrugged again, embarrassed. "You're just too damn appealing. It was a natural, automatic reaction." Well, here he was in a hole and he just couldn't stop digging, could he? "Look, I didn't grab *you.* You grabbed *me.* And I couldn't resist quickly enough."

Her eyes widened. "Oh, so now you're saying I threw myself at you?"

He hesitated, trying to evaluate just how much of her reaction was real anger, and how much plain nervousness with the entire situation. He thought he saw more of the latter and his wide mouth tilted into a slight grin, betting on her being receptive to a teasing response at this point. "Yeah. More or less."

"Out!" She pointed the way to the door, only now her fury was pretty obviously mostly playacting.

He looked down at her and shook his head, half laughing. "Okay, Annie. I think you've got everything you're going to need. I'll see you in the morning."

"If I'm still here."

"Right."

At the door he stopped and turned back. She stood looking at him. The anger in her face had melted away and she looked incredibly young and endearing, standing there in her nightgown and robe, her dark hair flying about her in an unruly cloud. He wanted to go back and gather her up in his arms and cradle her through the night.

Wincing, he pushed back the impulse, but he couldn't stop staring at her, wondering where this need to nurture had come from. He'd never had it before. He was good at doctoring, conscientious and talented. But he'd never had the deep sense of commitment to humanity he saw in some of his colleagues. He loved medicine, but it was a job, a career, an identity, not a mission. This was something new and he couldn't help but think it might be something dangerous.

Had it been a mistake to bring her here? No doubt. He was stuck with her now, like the old adage that said once you'd saved someone's life you were responsible for them from then on. He'd taken over her problems and he was now going to have to do something about fixing them. Maybe he should have minded his own business.

Too late for second thoughts. She was here and he was afraid he'd changed his destiny because of it.

"Sleep tight," he said.

"You too," she said so softly it was almost a whisper.

But it was the look in her eyes that he carried away with him.

"Matt? Is that you?"

His older sister Rita opened the door to her bedroom and peered out at him sleepily.

"What are you doing?"

"Nothing. Go back to bed. I'll talk to you in the morning."

She yawned. "Oh. Okay," she said dutifully, closing her door again.

He smiled as he went on toward his own bedroom down the hall. It was funny, but he almost resented that he had to share Annie with the rest of his family. He wasn't quite ready for that. She was a treasure, something he'd found that he wanted all to himself for now. Or maybe it was just that he didn't want to have to explain to everyone just exactly what it was that he was doing with her—why he wanted her in his office, why he couldn't stand to have her in that awful place she was living.

Because he wasn't too sure of that himself.

Chapter Four

Annie's eyes opened and she smiled dreamily. What a pleasure to wake up between these soft sheets in a room that looked as though it belonged to someone who was loved. That someone wasn't her—but it almost felt as though it could be.

She heard a door slam and her smile faded. Memories of Matt and his unexpected kiss flooded her. Challenges like that tended to leap out at the most unlikely moments. This was no time to let herself drift with the tide. She was actually in enemy territory of sorts and she was going to need to be on her toes.

She slipped out of the bed, reached for her robe and opened the door to the hall—just a crack at first to make sure no one else was in sight, then wide enough to let her glide down the carpeted walkway to the bathroom. Luckily, it was unoccupied and she let herself inside, closing the door firmly and looking in vain for a way to lock it. There was some sort of brass thingy but she couldn't figure out how to work it.

Oh, well. She shouldn't be in here long. Turning, she took a look at the place, taking in the bright shiny aqua tile, the huge Roman-style bathtub, the skylighted atrium, the three-sided mirror. And the space. The bathroom was about the size of her apartment.

"Very nice," she murmured with a sigh. She could get used to this sort of living. It was even going to be a pleasure brushing her teeth in this atmosphere. She only wished she had about three spare hours to make use of that great bathtub.

Sadly, there was only time to brush her teeth and she went to the marble pedestal sink, turning on the water from the golden faucet. It poured out like liquid silver and she loved watching it spill over her toothbrush. It also made quite a bit of noise and that was probably why she didn't hear the knock on the door. She was just energetically lathering up when the door opened and a bright young blond woman in a cherry red bathrobe came rushing in.

"Sorry Rita, I've got to—"

The young woman stopped dead, staring at Annie.

Annie tried to smile, but it felt a little silly considering she was foaming at the mouth like a mad dog.

"Oh," she said lamely, her voice coming out a bit muffled. "Hi."

"Oops," the blond girl said. "I'm sorry. I thought my sister was in here." She started to retreat, then her face changed and she came back in. "Uh, who are you exactly?"

"I'm Annie." Grabbing a washcloth, she quickly wiped most of the bubbles from her face. "Matt sort of—"

"Ah." She looked even more surprised, but raised a hand and started to back out again. "Say no more."

Annie took a step toward her. "No, really, I'd like to explain—"

The woman shook her head. "No need." She hesitated, a spark of humor appearing in her gaze. "I'm Jodie, by the way."

Annie smiled uncertainly. "Hi, Jodie. I'm Annie."

"Hi." Jodie looked to be in her late twenties, just about Annie's age, with shoulder-length blond hair and warm brown eyes. She had a friendly manner, but she was obviously still a little skeptical about this stranger in her bathroom. Her gaze dropped to take in the lacy nightgown and the obvious evidence of pregnancy. Her eyes widened. "I'll just leave you to…whatever."

"I'm just brushing my teeth." She waved the toothbrush in the air as proof positive.

"Uh-huh." Jodie's smile was tentative. "Where's Matt?"

Annie thought for a second, then shook her head. "I'm not sure."

"Oh." A slight frown was deepening between Jodie's eyebrows. "I'll just go look for him." She turned to go, but Annie stopped her.

"Wait!"

Jodie turned back with a questioning look.

"First of all, how do you use this lock?"

Jodie laughed. "I guess that would be good to know," she admitted, then showed her the trick to it.

"Great. Now…see, the thing is, I've got a problem." There was no way to soften the embarrassment, so she charged ahead frankly. "You see, I don't have any clothes."

Jodie blinked and swallowed. "Is that right?" she said in a shaky voice.

"Yes. If I could just borrow a few things…"

Jodie opened her mouth, then closed it again. She shook her head and when she spoke again, her voice was higher. "No problem. Uh…"

"Hey, Jodie?" called a male voice from the hallway.

Jodie looked torn. "It's David," she said worriedly.

"The younger brother." Annie remembered about him.

"Yes."

Annie smiled. Despite her own embarrassment, she couldn't help but have some empathy for Matt's little sister. She was obviously trying hard not to slight anyone here.

"Better answer him," she suggested.

Jodie nodded and a determined look came over her pretty face. "I guess so. I'll be right back." Turning, she slipped out the door.

Annie listened as she tried to explain to her brother what was going on.

"*Matt* brought her?" David said loud enough for her to hear. "Matt hasn't had a girlfriend for so long, I was starting to think he'd forgotten how this man-woman thing worked. I've got to see this."

"Shh," Jodie hissed at him. "You're not seeing anything. Get Rita."

"Rita?"

"Yes. Get her. Quick."

Jodie came back into the room, smiling brightly as she closed the door behind her. "Sorry about that. Now about those clothes you need…"

"Yes. Thanks, I really appreciate it. I could use a shirt and—" She looked down at her belly. "Maybe some stretchy pants. Something I can wear to work."

"Of course." She hesitated. "Where do you work?"

Annie laughed, resigning herself to the fact that everything she said was going to make this situation look crazier and crazier to any sane observer. "I know you'll find this hard to believe, but I'm supposed to start a new job at Allman Industries today. As your brother's assistant, actually."

"No kidding?"

Jodie laughed, too, obviously on the same wavelength, and Annie had a sudden intuition that they were going to be friends. As long as nothing came along to change the way Jodie felt about her.

"Jodie?" A new voice sounded outside the door, along with a light knock.

"That'll be Rita," Jodie said. "Mind if I…?" She gestured questioningly toward the door

Annie held up both hands. "Be my guest," she said with a touch of irony.

Jodie grinned and turned to let her sister into the bathroom. Annie noted wryly that it was a good thing the place was as large as the average living room. At this rate, it was filling fast.

"Rita, this is Annie. Matt brought her here."

The two of them exchanged significant glances.

"So David has been telling me."

Rita stuck out her hand and Annie shook it. She saw more of Matt in this sister. Just as blond, she was older than Jodie, not quite as slender, nor as pretty, with her hair pulled back in a got-no-time-for-nonsense ponytail. She had a calm, competent look about her. What she didn't look was pleased.

"So you're a friend of Matt's?"

This one wasn't going to be an automatic friend. Annie felt like an interloper again—like a child caught with her hand in the cookie jar and vamping hard to think of an excuse that would cover it.

"Sort of. Actually, we only got to know each other well yesterday. But he's been awfully kind and…uh…"

Enough already, she was telling herself. Stop. Don't let your nervousness make you say stupid things.

"Ah." Both sisters said it at the same time and both gazes dropped to glance at Annie's rounded belly at the same time as well. They were wondering about exactly how long she and Matt had been acquainted, even if not "really well."

Annie sighed. Obviously she was going to have to try to nip this suspicion in the bud. "Look…I think you people are getting the wrong idea about this," she began.

"Oh, we're not getting any ideas," Jodie denied brightly, shaking her head.

Rita waved a hand in the air but managed to sound just a bit sarcastic when she added, "Haven't had an idea since last Wednesday and I'm not likely to get new ones in the morning, anyway."

Annie appreciated their attempt to reassure her, but there was no point to it. She knew very well what they were thinking.

"I mean…Matt and I aren't…you know…"

"Yes?" They both waited expectantly.

Annie searched for the right word. "Together."

"Oh."

To her surprise, though Rita looked unconvinced, Jodie actually looked a little deflated, as though she'd been hoping there was a budding romance revealing itself. Why on earth, she thought, would she want her brother to be interested in a pregnant stranger he'd picked up off a café floor? Of course, they didn't know about that. But still…

"Hey."

All three of them jumped inches into the air, because this time it was Matt's voice outside the door.

"What's going on?" he called, sounding authoritative. They weren't going to be able to send him away the way they had David.

They looked at each other. Jodie was the first to move.

"Oh, what the heck," she said, surrendering to the inevitable. "Why don't you come on in, Matt? We're having a party in here."

"Is Annie in there with you?"

"Yes, I am," she called back fighting back a bubble of slightly hysterical laughter that was threatening to come up her throat. "Come on in. The more the merrier."

It seemed a simple thing to invite him in, but the moment he appeared in the doorway, a sense of her own vulnerability swept over her. She was so naked beneath the nightgown. Funny how that hadn't bothered her much the night before. Now, it did.

She pulled her robe in closer and she knew both women noticed the move. He stepped in, scowling at each one in turn as they gaped back at him, and the room seemed to shrink in size.

"What are you two looking at?" he growled at his sisters.

"Nothing," Rita said a bit defensively.

"Not a thing," Jodie echoed more innocently, her brown eyes wide.

He didn't buy it but he let it go. "I guess you've met Annie?"

"I guess we have," Jodie said, throwing a quick smile Annie's way. "We've gotten real close in a very short time. In fact, I'm planning on loaning her some clothes."

"Clothes?" Rita asked, startled.

"Yes. It seems Matt brought her here in her nightgown."

"What?" Rita's face registered horror.

Annie wanted to give the background but no one was listening to her. Jodie had a mischievous grin on her face and Rita was demanding an explanation from Matt, which he obviously resented.

"I'll talk to you about it later," he told his older sister sternly. "Right now, do you mind giving us a moment of privacy? I'm sure you have something else to do somewhere else in the house. Like the kitchen," he added pointedly.

"Sexist, ain't he?" Jodie gave Annie a look of pure exasperation. "Take that under advisement, my dear."

But Rita was frowning. "Matt, I don't know if that would be proper. I mean—"

"I know what you mean and I reject it." He jerked his head toward the door.

Annie watched, fascinated. Matt was so sure of himself, so certain of being obeyed by his sisters, that it was a sight to behold. She wondered how he'd trained them so well.

Jodie grabbed Rita's hand. "Come on, sis. Let's get out of here. I'm sure Matt knows what he's doing."

Rita didn't look convinced of that, but she allowed herself to be led out. Jodie called back over her shoulder, "I'll be back with those clothes in a few minutes."

"Thanks," Annie called after her as the door closed.

She looked up at Matt and wished he wasn't so darn handsome that it almost took her breath away every time she really let herself look at him. The dark hair was unruly at the moment, and his white shirt was left open at the neck revealing an impressive view of hard, tanned muscles. For some reason this brought up visions of tangled sheets on a wide bed and memories of his potent kiss. Before she could stifle it, her pulse was soaring.

There was no use trying to pretend otherwise—the man was a danger to her peace of mind. It was too early in the morning for this. Her defenses weren't up to speed. She swallowed hard and faced him.

"We've scandalized your sisters," she pointed out.

He shrugged, looking down at her with a wariness that seemed to be a part of him. "I didn't know that was possible. You learn something new every day."

She bit her lip, considering. "You may think it's a joke, but actually, I don't want to scandalize them."

"It's too late now. The deed's been done."

"No." She shook her head firmly, coming to a decision. "I agree with Rita. This is no time or place for this."

He looked perplexed. "I just want to go over some things with you. First of all, how do you feel? Any problems during the night?" He looked at her rounded belly peeking out from the robe and his face softened.

She was torn. On the one hand, she'd noticed that look on his face and it touched her. On the other, she had to stick to her guns here. There was no way she was going to start following orders the way his sisters did. Hesitating for only a split second, she made her decision.

Lifting her chin, she pointed to the door. "Out."

He stared at her, at a loss. "What are you talking about?"

She drew in her breath and looked up at him. Risky as it might be, she was opting for complete honesty. "I'm standing here practically naked and you're standing very close and we're alone. It's no good."

He shook his head, astounded at her attitude. "This is nuts. What do you think I'm going to do? Grab you and drag you off into the tub?"

"That's not the point."

He blinked at her stubbornness. "Well, you're the one who's 'practically naked,' as you put it. I'm fully clothed." One eyebrow rose. "So I guess you'd have to say the impropriety is all on your side."

She shook her head. She was not going to get sidelined by his attempts at humor. She'd been going along with most of what Matt wanted ever since she met him and it was time she began establishing a set of standards for their relationship. He had to know that she meant what she said when she said it. Otherwise, it would be too easy to let herself fall completely under his control. And that would be disastrous.

"You don't see that your sisters might find a private meeting in the bathroom a little strange?"

"Who cares what they think?"

"*I* care." She pointed at her own chest. "Me. This person right here."

"Annie…" He grabbed her hand and pulled her closer. "Listen."

He'd meant to use logic. A good argument was always useful. Words. Lots of words. But for some reason, words deserted him the moment he felt her warm hand in his and looked down into her dark-brown eyes. He'd had a case to make when he'd started, but it was gone now. He couldn't remember what he'd been talking about.

It was magic. He didn't speak and neither did she, but there was no urge to move along. He could have stayed there for days, just drowning in her gaze—no need for air or food or anything but her. It was very strange. He'd never felt this way with a woman before—as though he wanted to breathe her in until she was a part of his existence.

She broke out of the spell first. Pulling away, she drew in a sharp breath and pointed to the door.

"Out. You can talk to me after I'm done here. When I'm dressed."

For just a second or two, he was disoriented, not sure what was going on. And then he was outside the bathroom and she was locking the door. He stood there for a moment, digesting the situation, and slowly his equilibrium came back to him. But not his peace of mind. What the hell was going on? Was he losing his reason?

Walking down the hallway to his own bedroom, he rubbed the back of his neck with his hand and wondered what he'd gotten himself into. He hadn't bargained for a situation that involved his emotions this way. Every step he was taking seemed to be drawing Annie into his life more and more. It was all very well to keep insisting to himself that he was in this to protect her baby. The trouble was, Annie came along with it. And there he had to keep his distance.

Just as he reached his door, Rita called to him from her room across the hall.

"Hey there, brother. We need to talk."

Turning, he took in the flare of some sort of disquiet in her eyes and he indulged in a silent groan. "What is it?" he asked reluctantly.

She came out to meet him half way. "Look, Matt," she said firmly. "I'm really happy if you've found someone. We've all been really worried about you lately, not having a woman in your life and all." She glanced down the hall toward the bathroom and lowered her voice. "But to bring her here like this is just a bit much."

Matt bit his tongue and told himself to hold back the resentful words he was tempted to use. Rita was the oldest and since their mother had died years earlier, she had been the one who had raised them all. He loved her dearly and was grateful for all the work she'd put in over the years. But sometimes her inflexible manner was a pain in the neck. And this was one of those times.

"Rita, she's my patient," he said once he'd tamed his first impulse to snap at her. "If I feel the need to put a patient of mine up for a few days, I'm going to do it. I do apologize for not consulting the rest of you first, but it was one of those things. There was no time."

"Oh, please." She rolled her eyes, obviously not buying it. "Matt, really! It's only obvious that she is much more than a patient to you."

"Rita, what are you talking about? I'm Annie's doctor. I wanted her here so that I could keep a closer eye on her."

"Sure," she said, not buying a word of it. "I'll believe that when I see you carting old Mrs. Winterhalter over the threshold and into the bedroom beside yours next time she's got the gout. Just to keep an eye on her."

"Rita..."

"Oh, Matt, she's a very attractive woman and you're a very lonely man at the moment. Nothing could be more natural than for you to be interested in her. It's so obvious."

His frown deepened. "It may be obvious to you, but it hasn't sunk in for me yet," he protested evenly. "There is nothing serious going on between Annie Torres and me."

Rita blinked at him, then looked truly distressed. "Matt! You wouldn't bring a one night stand into your own home..."

No force in the world could keep the anger out of his voice now.

"No, of course not. Rita, be serious. Annie isn't my lover in any way, shape or form. Or maybe you didn't you notice? She just happens to be over six months pregnant."

She stared at him for a long moment, biting her lip. The apology he'd been expecting didn't materialize. Then she turned and headed for the stairs.

Matt swore softly to himself, annoyed but controlling it. Just barely. And then he followed her, determined to get her to see how wrong she was. Despite all appearances, he really did care what his family thought of him.

"Listen, Rita," he said as he found her in the kitchen, pulling a carton of eggs out of the refrigerator. "This is what you don't understand. Annie is…" He tried to think of a good comparison. "Think of her as a waif, a little match girl I found shivering in the snow."

Rita choked. "Matt, it's going to be ninety degrees today."

He fixed her with a steely gaze. "I'm using metaphors, Rita."

"Yes. And overblown ones at that." She cracked an egg into a bowl and reached for another. "So you're telling me you found her wallowing around in the snow in that nightgown? With no backup gear?"

"Actually, she dropped into a dead faint at my feet in the middle of Millie's Café."

"Oh. I see."

But of course, she didn't see at all. "What I mean is she was in trouble and she needs a place to stay."

She put down the whisk and stared at the eggs for a

moment, then turned and faced him. "I hope I can assume that you were in no way responsible for the 'trouble' she's in?"

His head went back. He felt as though she'd slapped him. His eyes narrowed. "Why is it impossible to talk to you today?"

"Maybe because I just walked into my bathroom and found a strange pregnant woman in a nightgown brushing her teeth in my sink."

"Rita, her being pregnant has nothing to do with me."

She looked at him steadily. "I hope that's true, Matt," she said softly. "But before we found out about that baby of yours, I would have bet my life against you being involved in anything like that. It does undermine my sense of being able to judge things as they really are."

His heart went cold. So that was it. Now that the whole family knew about his relationship with Penny Hagar they saw him in a new light. The realization hit him like a thunderbolt. He'd always been the oldest brother, the one everyone turned to for wise counsel. He was the role model, the one his father trusted most, the one everyone admired. Was that really all gone now?

He turned from his sister. What more was there to say? If she didn't trust him now, what was the point of making excuses and pleading for understanding? He felt like an outsider in his own home. The only person he wanted to see right now was Annie. And that was just plain wrong.

His cell phone rang. Pulling it out, he glanced at the number in the window, knowing it would be Dan Kramer, the private investigator searching for his baby.

"Any news?" he said without preamble.

Dan talked quickly, but his words rang hollow. There was nothing new. Every lead seemed to peter out.

"Keep trying," he told the man as he signed off.

Keep trying. That advice could apply to every part of his life right now.

Annie drew in her breath and held it for a few seconds, then glanced at Matt sitting beside her in the driver's seat of his car. They were turning into the parking lot at Millie's Café and for some reason she was nervous.

"You'll enjoy it," Matt told her gruffly. "Relax. You'll have someone serving *you* breakfast for a change."

That was hardly the point. She felt odd, as though she were playacting in a scene for which she didn't know the lines. She'd just begun to feel comfortable about being in the Allman house when Matt had whisked her away.

Jodie had brought her a stack of clothes to pick from and she'd chosen dark-blue slacks with a soft and stretchy elastic waistband and a long white overshirt that was a little snug around her swollen breasts, but basically did the job she needed done. Matt assured her he would have someone clean out her apartment and bring everything over to the Allman house by that evening, so she would have her own clothes again. She wasn't sure she was crazy about that idea, but she had to admit she really didn't want to go back to her own place again if she didn't have to. Still, what would his sisters think?

Jodie was friendly and seemed welcoming enough. It was Rita who worried her. But when she'd come downstairs, Matt's oldest sister had smiled at her and begun to show her some of the many projects they were working on in preparation for Matt's brother Rafe's wedding to Shelly Sinclair. She'd been intrigued by the wide variety of supplies including yards and yards of white lace and chiffon, vats of seed pearls and spools of satin ribbon that littered the dining room table. She loved artsy-craftsy things.

But the next thing she knew, Matt was hurrying her out the door as though he didn't want her to spend another moment with his family. Which was too bad. She'd liked his sisters and she'd been ready to get to know them both better.

But he'd reminded her that they needed to pick up her car in the parking lot of the café, and she needed to tell Millie she wouldn't be working there any longer. So, reluctantly, she'd come along to have breakfast in the place where she used to work.

She wasn't sure exactly why she was dreading this, but it came clear to her pretty quickly when two women she knew casually came out of the café just as she and Matt were entering. She nodded with a quick smile and they each murmured greetings, then took in her escort, eyes widening. Identical looks came into both their faces and they glanced at each other meaningfully.

Annie could read their minds.

Aha. How do you like this? So Annie caught herself a live one, did she? Good for her.

Good for her, indeed! She hated seeming to be dependent on anyone other than herself. She wanted to tell them, *No! This is not what it looks like.*

But maybe she was wrong. Maybe it was exactly that.

Nails digging into her palms, she lifted her chin and walked into the café. Matt held the door for her, scanning the place for a sign of Millie. Nina Jeffords, one of Annie's favorites, was the hostess for the morning shift. She looked startled to see her co-worker coming in with Matt Allman, but she resisted the sort of cat-that-ate-the-canary expression Annie abhorred and showed them to a booth along the side.

"Millie's in her office," she told them. "Going over accounts. I would stay away if I were you," she added with a grin. "At least until she's got the books balanced."

"I'm afraid I'm going to have to risk having my head bitten off," Matt said with answering humor. "I've got some things I need to talk to her about." He helped Annie into her seat and turned. "Just coffee and scrambled eggs for me, Nina." He glanced down at Annie. "I'll go knock on Millie's door. You hold down the fort. Okay?"

Annie nodded. If he wanted to explain to Millie that she was losing one of her employees on such short notice, he might as well be her guest. She would have to explain herself soon enough and she wasn't looking forward to it. Maybe he would soften the way for her.

She watched him walk across the room, greeting various other customers as he went. And why not? Everyone in town knew the Allmans. Was that what made him look like small-town royalty? Maybe. Whatever. All she knew was, it made her shiver, and that was darn annoying.

Just before he reached the door to the hallway that led to Millie's office, he turned and found her watching him. She gasped softly as his piercing gaze caught hers and held for another beat. Then he turned again and was gone.

She sank back into her seat, breathing again and shaking her head. This was no good. She couldn't let this sort of thing happen. He was going to get the wrong idea.

"Annie." A hand fell on her shoulder. "I was hoping I'd find you here."

Chapter Five

Annie looked up with a start. Josh McLaughlin stood smiling down at her, his eighteen-month-old baby in his arms. She glanced back at where Matt had disappeared, glad he was out of sight. A meeting between McLaughlins and Allmans could turn into another shootout at the OK Corral. Then she turned the full force of her smile on Josh and reached to take his baby from him.

"Hey there, puddin'," she cooed. The adorable little girl had a pudgy body just made for cuddling and a head full of auburn curls that tumbled around her sunny face. "I've been missing you all week."

Josh laughed and little Emily McLaughlin gurgled happily and reached out a little hand to try to grab Annie's nose.

"You're not working today?" Josh asked her.

She looked up, assessing the man who she was pretty

sure was her half brother, but didn't know it. Tall and slender as a long-distance runner, his dark-blond hair looked like he'd lost his comb in a windstorm. It always looked that way, no matter how much Cathy, his wife, coaxed and pleaded.

"I'm a rancher," he'd say, dropping a kiss on his wife's comically distressed face. "Just be glad there's no hay sticking out of my ears."

Annie loved watching the two of them together. Cathy was the perfect foil for him with her short, stylish cap of strawberry-blond hair and her impeccable taste in clothing, despite spending most of her time working out in the open alongside her husband. She was an excellent horsewoman and raising Arabians was becoming the specialty at the McLaughlin Ranch these days. They made a good team, but more than that, they made a good family. Their relationship went a long way toward restoring Annie's faith that real love wasn't an illusion, that it could last, if carefully nourished. And Emily, the baby, fit into the circle of their devotion perfectly. It was a joy to work for them.

She'd been so nervous driving out to the ranch on the day she'd answered their ad. Landmarks sparked memories, making it even worse. In some ways, she had been going home. But it was a home that might not want her. And she hadn't been sure what she was going to do once she got there. Would she announce straight out to Josh that they shared a father? Or would she go ahead with her plan to apply for the job and see what happened? Would he take one look at her and know the truth?

Oh, hardly. If it had been that obvious, someone else

would have noticed by now and no one had come close. But what if they hadn't liked her, or she couldn't stand them? They could have ordered her off the premises.

Her knees had been shaking as she'd knocked on the door. She held her breath as she heard footsteps coming closer. And then the door had opened and Josh looked out at her. He hadn't exactly recognized her or seen the signs of siblinghood, but there definitely had been an instant connection—though not in the romantic sense. He'd grinned and thrown the door wide and she knew before he said anything that she was hired on the spot.

Now she wondered if he ever noticed the similarities between them. She detected new ones all the time. Like the way his mouth twisted to one side when he grinned. She did that, too. Didn't he see it? Did he ever look into her eyes and wonder…?

No, that was silly. He had no reason to suspect anything at all. No reason in the world. And what was he going to think once she told him the truth? She shied away from speculating about it. Their relationship was so good right now, she didn't want to do anything to risk ruining it. Not yet.

"Actually, I'm not going to be working here at all anymore," she told Josh, cuddling Emily close. "I may be starting a new job."

He raised an eyebrow. "Are you still going to be able to work for us on Thursdays?" he asked, looking concerned.

"Absolutely," she said, though she hadn't brought it up to Matt yet and didn't know what was going to happen once he realized it was Josh she was working for.

"Great," he said, looking relieved as he reached to take his baby back. "I just dropped by on our way to the feed store, hoping to catch you here, because Cathy wanted me to ask if you could come an hour early this week. She's hoping you'll be able to help her take Emily to Groban's Studios for a portrait sitting."

"That sounds like fun."

"Oh, yeah." He grimaced. "Better you than me."

Annie laughed. "Emily will come alive in front of the camera. Won't you punkin'?"

Emily gurgled happily and Josh made her wave goodbye.

"See you Thursday," he said back over his shoulder as he headed for the door.

"Bye."

With impeccable timing, Matt appeared at the table, but his gaze was on Josh's back.

"Isn't that Josh McLaughlin?" he asked gruffly.

She nodded.

"I didn't know you knew him." He frowned, looking just the way she would expect an Allman to look when a McLaughlin was around. And vice versa. "What did he want?"

Luckily Nina arrived with coffee and scrambled eggs for two and Annie was saved from having to answer that. It was a question that needed answering, but she wasn't ready just yet. The baby was kicking, leaving her a little breathless, and she put a hand over where the little leg seemed to be jutting out, hoping to quiet it.

"Did you talk to Millie?" she asked, changing the

subject as he slid onto the seat across from her and they settled down to eat.

"Yes. I told her. She was sorry to lose you, of course, but she understood, especially after what happened yesterday. And she wishes you well." He buttered his golden-brown slice of toast. "She'd like you to stop in and see her at some point today."

"Of course. I planned to do that."

"Just don't let her try to talk you into anything."

Annie looked up at him. Conflicting emotions were tugging her in all directions. She liked the man. But she was so wary of letting herself depend on him.

She wished she knew why he was being so nice to her. With any other man she would have been suspicious. And in fact, she had her moments last night when he'd carted her off into the dark. But now—despite the kiss they'd shared the night before, she was pretty sure it wasn't anything like that.

Was he just superdoc, concerned with her baby and determined to make sure she ate right and did what she could to start the child off well in the world? Maybe there was a little of that. But there was something else going on, something deeper, something that struck an emotional chord with him. And she thought it might have something to do with what she'd told him about considering adoption for her baby. That seemed to give him fits every time she brought it up. Was he going to try to talk her out of it?

That was just the problem. She couldn't let herself get into a position of doing what other people thought she ought to do, just because she felt grateful to them.

She was going to stay true to herself, even if that meant turning away from Matt and rejecting his help.

"You know, Matt," she started carefully. "I appreciate all you're doing for me. But I'll be the one to decide what I'm going to do. I'm coming in with you to see how this job you're offering me looks. But I'm not making any promises. I may decide not to take it. I may just have to look for something else."

He stared back at her, reining in his impulse to snarl with displeasure. Didn't she understand that everything he was doing was for her own good? And the good of her baby? Did she really question his motives?

But no. Once he'd calmed down enough to really see what was going on in her dark gaze, he began to realize the truth. She was wary. Scared, even. She'd been hurt in the past and she didn't want to risk trusting anyone right now. Yelling at her wasn't going to change that much. In fact, it would probably just make things worse.

Looking at her, he made himself relax. There was something in her that really touched him. She seemed so small and vulnerable, and that was exactly what she was. Pregnant and all alone. But so brave, so firmly standing up for what she thought she ought to. It reached in to his heart and made him smile. And it made him think about Penny.

"Annie." He reached across the table and took her hand, surprising her as much as he surprised himself by the move. "Tell me about your baby's father. What happened?"

She stared at him and suddenly, her eyes filled with tears.

"Oh, damn!" she said, grabbing a napkin with her free hand to sop up the moisture. "I don't ever do this. I never, ever cry."

"Cry all you want," he told her, his fingers curling around hers. "We're in a corner booth. You're not that visible. And if you need to cry…"

"No," she said, jerking her hand away from his and glaring at him soggily. "Don't give me any sympathy, darn it all. Don't you see? That's exactly what's making me cry."

Leaning back, he laughed softly. "Okay. No more sympathy from me. I promise."

Taking a deep, shaky breath, she looked up at him. "Good. Just watch your step." She cleared her throat, blinking rapidly, trying to smile.

He looked down at his food to keep from grinning at her too broadly. "Listen, Annie. Forget I asked. If you can't talk about it—"

"I can talk about it," she said stoutly. "Just give me a moment." She took a sip of coffee and settled back, looking up at him defiantly. "Okay. Here goes. I was in nursing school when I met Rick. We bumped into each other in the cafeteria. Literally. My lemon gelatin dessert went all over the tiled floor."

He nodded as she paused. She had the look of someone going back into time, waiting to see if it still felt the same. He liked the fact that she was doing this right, not just shrugging it off with a caustic word or two as he might have expected. He realized with a jolt that he had an insatiable desire to get to know her better—her background, where she came from, why she did the things she did.

Why was that? He wasn't sure, but he was very much afraid it had a lot to do with the fact that he couldn't get the memory of what her mouth had tasted like the night before out of his mind. Wincing, he shook the thought away and listened as she went on.

"Rick helped me clean up the mess and we laughed about it. Then he insisted on taking me out to a real meal in a nice restaurant to make up for it." A slight smile played at her lips as the memories came to her. "He was so different from any man I'd ever known before. I fell for him the way a brainless teenager falls for the first boy that kisses her." Sighing, she gave him a plaintive glance. "Looking back now, I see how pathetic it was."

"Falling in love is a natural thing to do."

"Sure. But one should try to avoid falling for jerks. And I should have seen the signs." Her eyes took on a faraway look again as she remembered. "He was so handsome. I'd seen him around before. I knew about him. The girls in the nursing program were always being warned to watch out for the male med students. Which only made them seem more appealing, of course."

"Of course."

Picking up her coffee cup, she cradled it in her hands and took a long sip before going on.

"He was so interesting. His conversation was full of talk of European trips and yachts and famous people. It was another world, a world I'd never known before. I was mesmerized by it. I couldn't believe that someone like him was paying attention to someone like me." Her lips took on a faint smile again. "He had a way of leaning close and studying your face as he talked to you. It made you feel as though you were the only person he cared about in all the world." Her short laugh was humorless. "And actually, I'm sure his mind was a million miles away."

Matt nodded, feeling sympathetic, but a little annoyed at the same time. The guy sounded like a con man to him. He would have thought a smart woman like Annie would have seen through his act quickly enough to protect herself.

"There are politicians like that," he said gruffly.

"So I've heard. I've probably voted for some of them. Because I sure fell for Rick's act."

He waited for a moment. She was silent, staring down at her hands on the vinyl tabletop. "Were you in love with him?" he asked at last, wondering if she noticed the gritty sound to his voice as he said it.

She hesitated and suddenly his heart was beating harder. *What the hell? Did he really care this much? What was wrong with him?*

"I thought I was," she said at last. "I really did." She looked up at him, her gaze open and completely candid. "But you know, it's funny. As soon as he looked at me with that cold hardness in his eyes and told me to get rid of the baby or he wasn't interested in seeing me again, it was like this whole fantasy exterior melted away and I saw him as he really was. I saw the real Rick." She made a face. "And that was someone I didn't even like. And when he said to me that his family would hire private detectives who could prove that he wasn't the only one I'd been with…" Her voice choked off and the tears threatened again. Tears of anger.

Matt's mouth tightened. "What a bastard," he said with icy calm. "Maybe I should pay him a little visit and—"

"No! No, that would be crazy."

She stared at him, startled by how quickly he came to her defense. He shouldn't do that. They didn't have that sort of a bargain here.

"And anyway, what makes you so sure he wasn't right about that?" she asked softly, searching his face for her answer.

He didn't hesitate. The answer was right on the surface of his thinking. "Because I know you," he said simply.

She shook her head slowly, feeling a sense of wonder threaded with a hint of apprehension. "No, you don't."

Staring right back, he didn't retreat. "Yes, I do."

For some reason, that choked her up again. She fumbled for a napkin and Matt threw some cash down on the table.

"Come on," he said gruffly, "let's go."

"Oh, I need to go back and see Millie."

"We can do that later."

Later sounded good. She really didn't want to have to make happy talk with someone else right now. She let him lead her out of the café and into the parking lot. She didn't have much resistance left at the moment. Unburdening herself of her story had exhausted her.

"We'll come back for lunch," he suggested as he led her toward the cars. "You can see Millie then."

She glanced at him sideways. He kept saying "we." She had to conjure up enough energy to nip this in the bud at least.

He'd parked his low-slung sports car next to her beat-up old economy sedan. As they approached the cars, she couldn't help but notice the symbolism there. He waited while she unlocked the door to her car, then turned and faced him.

"We're not a *we,*" she said, forcing herself to confront him.

He looked at her, startled. "What?"

"We're not a *we.* In fact, we're not even a *you and me.* I'm Annie Torres and you're Matt Allman, and I'm me and you are you. Two separate people. Not *we.*"

"Oh." His face cleared as he got it. "I agree with you. Absolutely. That's the way it's got to be."

She nodded and he looked a bit sheepish.

"Sorry. I'll try not to let my language get that sloppy again."

"Okay. That'll be fine, then." She got into the driver's seat, wishing he weren't standing there watching. It was an awkward thing to do with this huge baby in the way.

"See you in the parking lot at Allman Industries," she said out the window she'd opened as she pulled on her seat belt and put her key into the ignition. To her relief, the engine roared to life. It didn't always cooperate that easily. She put the car into Reverse. He was still standing there, watching her. "Last one there is a rotten egg," she said, and then added, "Bye loser," before heading out.

She saw his frown of consternation as she drove out of the lot before he even got his car door open. "Don't worry," she murmured as though to the man who couldn't possibly hear her. "I'm not going to drive too fast. I'm going to take very good care of this baby. You just wait and see."

The inside of the Allman Industries building was as musty and old-fashioned as the outside looked but it was buzzing with activity. The energy of success was in the air.

And there was something else. Annie could feel it. It took some time for her to realize what it was, but when she did, it made a lot of other things fall into place for her. The simple truth was that the spirit of Jesse Allman, Matt's father, was baked into the bones of the place. She hadn't seen him here and she hadn't seen him at the house back on Alamo Road, but his presence was a constant in both places. You might almost say he haunted the buildings. She'd heard about him all her life and she remembered seeing him when she was a girl. He'd loomed large, even then.

He was, after all, the enemy of her father, William McLaughlin. She'd never been sure if she was supposed to align herself with Jesse out of anger toward her father for ignoring her, or against him because of solidarity with her family. Different years she felt differently. Now she thought she could stand back and look at it all more objectively, and she'd decided they both were a couple of jerks from a generation where men who did big things thought they could be kings.

But Matt wasn't like that. Or, if he was, he was hiding it. She felt a sudden gratitude and thought she'd better express it before it passed away.

"Matt," she said, slipping a hand into the crook of his arm as they entered the building. "I know I'm sort of…well, prickly sometimes, and I just wanted you to know that I really appreciate what you're doing for me."

He smiled and shrugged. "I should thank *you.*"

She blinked. "What for?"

"You woke me up to thinking about someone other than myself for a change. We're both going to do anything we can for that baby in there," he said, nodding toward her belly. "But in the meantime—" he glanced around the lobby "—what exactly can you do?"

She looked around, too. "I told you. I was training to be a nurse."

He grimaced. "How about typing?"

"Minimal."

"That's okay. The hunt and peck style will do for now. There's not that much typing to be done." He nodded and smiled at the main lobby receptionist. "What I mainly need is schedule organization. And a lot of fielding of phone calls. Setting up meetings. Coordinating with my other office staff."

"I think I can handle that."

"Good."

Matt gave her a quick tour of the building, introducing her to a few people along the way, and ended up in his own offices which were on the first floor toward the back in an out-of-the way corridor. The accommodations were plain but newly refurbished and modern. She would have a large desk which sat in the front room. His own setup was in another office that opened off the room where she would be working. It took no time at all for her to familiarize herself with the computer, printers, copying machine and the phone system. Then a call came in and Matt was needed in another area of the plant.

"You'll be okay?" he asked her.

"Of course," she told him, relieved to get some time alone. "Go to your meeting."

She could tell he was leaving reluctantly and she sighed. If their plans were going to work out, he was going to have to get over this right away. Funny, but she didn't worry as much about herself. She'd been through the fires before and she'd learned her lesson. Shaking herself, she rose and went to the file cabinet. There was no quicker way to learn what went on in an office than to try to straighten out the files.

She was still at it almost an hour later when a pretty young woman with sleek blond hair peeked in.

"Annie!"

She looked up and saw Millie's daughter in the doorway. She'd met her a number of times at the café and knew she was the one about to marry Matt's younger brother, Rafe.

"Shelley! Come on in."

Shelley stepped in, looking around the office. "I heard about you working here now. This will be great. We'll have to do lunch one of these days."

"Definitely."

Shelley turned and smiled at her and it seemed to Annie that she was radiating joy. Being engaged seemed to agree with her.

"I know my mother will miss you at the café," she said. "She's always talking about what a good waitress you are. Nothing but compliments."

"I love your mother. She's wonderful to work for. But with the baby getting closer…"

"Oh, yes, an office job is much better for you at this point. No doubt about it." There was a sound out in the hallway and her smile broadened. "Want to meet Rafe?" she said in a loud whisper. "My fiancé."

Annie laughed. From the eager manner in which she asked the question, there was no way to turn her down. She knew Rafe was acting as CEO of the company during his father's illness—despite the fact that Matt was the oldest and their father's choice for the top job. And she had heard that Shelley had recently been promoted right out of the administrative assistant pool into a management job as head of research and development planning. This was, by all rights, a high-powered couple. Impressive.

"Sure," she said in answer to Shelley's offer to meet her fiancé. "I'd love to."

Shelley went to the door and called to him. "Come on in and meet Annie Torres."

The man who entered the office didn't look much like Matt. There was a dark and untamed quality to him that startled Annie a little. But his knowing smile as they shook hands dispelled her unease right away.

"So you're the little lady who's creating such a sensation around the Allman house," he said, raising an eyebrow. "You've got the place in a dither. I've been getting phone calls all morning."

She was blushing. This was crazy! She never blushed. But then, she didn't cry, either. This had been a day for firsts.

"I think you're overstating it a little," she protested.

"Oh, believe me, I've heard all about you and Matt."

That put her back up right away. "There is no 'me and Matt.' Everyone is getting the wrong idea about this. His interest in me is purely—" she patted her rounded belly for emphasis "—professional. In the medical sense."

"Oh," Rafe said with a crooked grin. "Sure it is." He and Shelley exchanged a glance. "Well, it's nice to meet you, Annie Torres. I'm sure we'll be seeing more of you. Shelley is over at the house all the time, getting ready for the wedding."

"And Rafe is over at the house all the time, just because he wants to be," Shelley added in a teasing voice. "Makes you wonder why he bothered getting an apartment since he never seems to use it."

"Oh, it has its uses," he teased right back, sliding an arm around her waist and pulling her close before dropping a kiss at her temple.

She giggled and they started toward the door.

"We'll let you get back to work," Shelley said over her shoulder. "But we'll be seeing a lot of each other, I'm sure."

Annie waved goodbye and turned back to the files, but she heard another comment as they left the room.

"Get a load of those dimples," Rafe said sotto voce to Shelley. "Matt always did go for girls with dimples."

"Shh," Shelley said back.

And then they were gone.

Annie stood frozen to the spot. She was beginning to feel like a winded fish swimming against the tide. What was wrong with everyone?

Don't let it get to you, a voice inside warned. *They're not serious. They're giddy. That's what people are like when they're madly in love. And they want everyone else to be just as demented as they are.*

Madly in love. How would that be? Even when she'd thought she loved Rick, it wasn't quite like that. She was more in awe of him, impressed by him, flattered that he was interested in her. But love? No, it was never really love and she'd been a fool to give in to having a physical relationship with a man she didn't really love.

When you came right down to it, she'd never been in love. To love was to lay yourself open to a lot of risk. Even not being in love, she'd done that. She'd only come close, just touched the edges of what love could be, and even so, she'd paid the price. She'd been slapped in the face. No, it was best to keep things at the level of respect. Love was for people who could afford it. And she'd never been one to squander what little she had on the frivolous.

The baby kicked and she relaxed, whispering sweet nothings as she patted the spot. Work. That was what she needed. Back to the files. She couldn't let herself dwell on Matt or on the expectations of others.

Actually, the job turned out to be fairly interesting. Annie liked bringing order to chaotic situations, so she enjoyed setting up a new filing system for incoming messages and reorganizing the office so that traffic flow was smoother. Immersing herself in her work, Annie had lost track of time when Matt returned from his meeting.

"Hello there. Anything happening?"

She looked up to see Matt smiling down at her. She smiled brightly in return, determined to keep things on a businesslike level.

"Well, let's see. You've had three calls. And you've got a meeting with the hospital board at three o'clock. Oh, and Rita wants you to call your father as soon as possible. He's worried about the Nunez contract."

He groaned. "He thinks if he can get me involved in negotiating that contract, I'll be tied up here for the rest of my natural life," he said. Glancing around the office, he looked surprised. "This place already looks different. What did you do?"

"Nothing much. Just a little dusting. A little straightening up. I moved a chair here, some files there."

He nodded approvingly. "Whatever it is, keep notes. You'll have to give pointers to Maureen for when she gets back."

Annie laughed. "Oh, right. That's just what she'll want—the temp worker to give her pointers on how to do her job better."

"If the shoe fits," he said, heading for his own office to leave his briefcase. "Listen, it's past time for lunch. You ready to go?"

She hesitated. This was exactly one of those places where she should be carefully pointing out to him that they weren't a couple. "You know, I can get myself over to Millie's," she noted.

He stopped, turning back. "You don't want to go to lunch with me?"

His eyes were huge as though it was going to hurt his feelings if she turned him down.

She stared, then threw her hands out. "Matt, don't do this to me."

"Don't do what?"

"Don't put me in this position. We can't be doing things together all the time." She shook her head, at a loss. "People...people will..."

"People will say we're in love?" he teased her.

"Hardly." He was making her laugh again and that was always fatal. "But Matt, you're my boss, not my boyfriend. We should act accordingly."

He sat looking down at her, all tough-guy and stubborn. "And as your boss, I'd like to take you to lunch to celebrate your first day at work."

"Matt—"

"In fact, I insist."

She shook her head, more in surrender than anything else. And deep down she knew it was more because she wanted to please him than because she felt pressured. Red lights should have been flashing. Alarms should have been going off. She was giving in to temptation.

"I swear I won't make you go to lunch again any time this whole week," he promised extravagantly.

"What about next week?" she muttered, still clinging to a modicum of rebellion. "That is, if there is a next week."

He raised an eyebrow. "Expecting Armageddon?" he teased.

She tossed her hair and looked up at him a touch of hostility in her eyes. "Who knows? You might fire me by then."

"I wouldn't risk any money on that," he advised, his eyes crinkling at the corners. "And in the meantime, let's go eat. Okay?"

She made him wait a moment longer, but finally she relented and reached for her purse. "Oh, okay. But really, Matt. We have to be more careful about how we come across to others."

He threw her an exasperated look. "Why do you care so much what others think?"

Raising her chin, she looked steadily into his eyes. "I have to. I've spent a lifetime fighting what other people think about me. It matters. It can make a big difference."

Something changed in his gaze and he reached for her. "Annie—"

"And one more thing," she said, deftly pushing his hand aside and evading his touch. "About my decision."

"Your decision?"

"Yes. About whether or not I'm going to work for you."

"Ah, that decision."

"I've decided I'd like to take the job. But I have to have Thursday afternoons off."

"Thursdays? What for?"

"That's the day..." She took a deep breath and pressed on. It was time to come clean about this. He deserved it. "That's the day I work out at the McLaughlin Ranch."

Chapter Six

The room turned deadly silent for a long moment while Matt digested what Annie had said. When he spoke again, his voice had an edge to it.

"What are you talking about?"

"I told you. I work as a housekeeper one day a week."

"Yeah, but you didn't tell me it was with the McLaughlins."

"Well, it is."

He rose from the desk and began pacing the floor. Stopping to stare out the window at one point, he raked his fingers into his thick hair, making it stand up on end. Then he turned back to challenge her.

"Are you telling me you think you can work for me and the McLaughlins at the same time?"

"Of course I can."

She was going to have to go on the offensive. If she

hung back and waited for him to be logical, she was going to lose the advantage and end up apologizing—or worse, agreeing not to go out to Josh and Cathy's anymore. And she had to maintain her contact with the McLaughlins at all costs. But of course, she couldn't tell Matt why. And without her reasoning, she knew this was going to be hard for him to understand.

"I can and I will."

He looked tortured. "But—"

"But what? You think I'm a spy?" She glared at him. "I thought you could see right down into my soul and knew what sort of person I was." She sighed. "Ah, but now you're wondering, can I really trust her?"

"Trust has nothing to do with it."

"So it mainly boils down to irrational hatred?"

He groaned, shaking his head. "You don't know what you're talking about, Annie. When we have some time to spare, I'll tell you things that will change your mind."

She rose, purse in hand. "No need. I've made my decision. If you can't handle me working for the McLaughlins, I'll have to look for another job. Or go back to Millie's."

He shook his head as he joined her, and there was no sign of any softening in his face.

"We'll talk. Over lunch. Let's go."

They did talk over lunch, but not about the McLaughlins. Annie saw Millie and they had a tearful embrace. And for the rest of the hour, patrons came by their table to wish her well and tell her how much they were going to miss her.

"I'm not actually going anyplace, you know," she said at last. "I'll be right here in town, working at Allman Industries. Anyone who wants to can easily give me a call."

"But it won't be the same as finding you here every day when I stop by for my usual patty melt," Katy Brewster complained. "I swear, your smile just lights up my day."

Annie was pleased and gratified—and very surprised that she seemed to make a difference in so many lives. After all, she hadn't been around all that long. But she enjoyed the compliments, and even more, she enjoyed the look in Matt's eyes as he watched all this.

"Quite the belle of the ball, aren't you?" he murmured to her as they were rising to leave and people were calling from across the restaurant to say goodbye. "Maybe we ought to run you for mayor."

He was being careful not to touch her or stand too close or in any way give off the sense that they had anything going on between the two of them. She appreciated his efforts. Still, she knew very well that people would make up their own minds about what was going on, even if she and Matt tried not to give them overt reason.

He helped her into the car and she waved at the last well-wishers, and then was relieved when they hit the highway and she could relax.

"Let's swing out by the new plant," Matt suggested when they reached the crossroads. "Have you ever been out there?"

"No. Actually, I haven't been out in that direction at all." Her heart started thumping. There was a reason she didn't go to that side of town and he was obviously about to suggest they go there. But if he stuck to the highway, they would bypass Coyote Park, the site of her childhood summers. She knew she was being a ninny avoiding it anyway. There was no reason for it.

Who's afraid of Coyote Park?

The taunt was silly enough to make her smile.

"Want to see the new building?" he asked, as she'd known he would.

She hardly hesitated. "Sure."

She'd heard a lot about the new site. Everyone said it was going to be a spectacular new setting for Allman Industries, and from what she saw as Matt slowly drove her around the construction area, they were right. The perimeters had been blocked off and the foundations laid. Very soon a tall building of steel and tinted glass would stand in the middle of what had always been a barren field. The Allmans were moving forward, grabbing the future and making it theirs. She was impressed.

"Stick with us and you'll be working out here by this time next year," Matt said. His deep voice sounded a bit cynical and she looked at him quickly, wondering why. But his eyes were crinkling at the corners and she might have mistaken humor for something more sarcastic.

"How about you?" she asked, curious now. "Will you still be with the company?"

The humor faded from his face. "That all depends," he said evasively, staring out at the structure.

"Depends on what?" she pursued.

She knew Matt had gone away to school partly to get away from his father. Everyone knew that. And he'd taken on the awesome effort of becoming a fully qualified

An Important Message from the Editors

Dear Reader,

If you'd enjoy reading romance novels with larger print that's easier on your eyes, let us send you TWO FREE HARLEQUIN ROMANCE® NOVELS in our LARGER-PRINT EDITION. These books are complete and unabridged, but the type is set about 25% bigger to make it easier to read. Look inside for an actual-size sample.

By the way, you'll also get a surprise gift with your two free books!

Pam Powers

Peel off Seal and Place Inside...

physician. From what she'd heard, he'd only come home and gone to work at Allman's a few months before because of his father's illness. He'd made a point of opening a medical office as well, just to emphasize the fact that he wasn't giving up on practicing medicine. But he'd said himself that his father was working hard to get him to take over the company instead.

"You never know what fate has in store for you," he said, giving her a quick smile. "Look at the way you fell into my life."

"*Fell* is the operative word," she noted. "No conscious effort on my part. Nothing I can claim credit for."

"You mean to tell me that fainting at my feet wasn't a nefarious plan concocted by you from the beginning? You weren't out to steal my heart by playing with my sympathies?"

She looked at him sharply just to make sure he was only joking. If he really thought anything like that, she would have even more reason to get out of his life immediately. But the humor flashing in his eyes told her he was teasing and she relaxed.

"If only I were smart enough to come up with such a plan," she said with mock wistfulness. "You are such a patsy."

"Am I?"

Of course the answer to that was no, but she wasn't going to give him the satisfaction of saying it out loud. Besides, the teasing was getting them too warm and cozy and she purposefully turned away. He got the message and turned the car back out onto the driveway, driving slowly up to a different vantage point.

"Matt," she said, frowning slightly. "Here's what I don't understand. If you don't want to work in business, and you do want to practice medicine, why can't you just tell your father what the facts are? Why waste all this time pretending?"

He laughed softly. "You make it sound so simple," he said. "So simple and so easy. And I suppose it would be for many people. But they don't have Jesse Allman for a father."

"Is he really that autocratic?"

"Oh, he's autocratic all right. But that's not how he gets you. It's the emotional blackmail. The guilt."

"Guilt? What do you have to be guilty about?"

"Life. You know how it is. Sometimes you feel guilty for things you've done, sometimes for things you haven't done—sometimes for loving too much, sometimes for loving too little. You know?"

She shook her head. She really didn't think she did know. After all, she'd never had a father to make her life miserable. She'd never had a father at all. So it was hard for her to sympathize. But it didn't matter. He'd started the car moving again.

"Let's take the old road back," he suggested.

The old road went right past the park. She bit her lip. *What the heck. It would be good to see the old place.*

She didn't have to wait long. They passed a couple of farms and then there it was: Coyote Park. It looked dusty and windswept, with a few stands of straggly-looking cottonwoods and junipers here and there, just as she remembered it. But one thing was different. She didn't see any people.

"Stop," she said suddenly. "Just for a minute. Please stop."

He pulled over, looking at her curiously. She got out of the car and looked around. She didn't dread this place. What had she been thinking? All sorts of childhood memories flooded back.

"Do you have a little time? Mind if I just go down there?" She pointed toward a rickety wooden bridge that still stood guard over the old rocky creek.

"No problem," he said.

Turning, she began to walk toward the bridge. Getting out of the car as well, he followed a few feet behind her.

"What is it, Annie?" he asked as she stepped onto the bridge and turned slowly, taking in everything.

She looked at him, knowing that to tell him her story would be to lower her respect quotient. But what the heck. It was only the truth. And somehow she realized she trusted Matt not to despise her for it as some might.

"This is where we camped sometimes in the summer when I was a kid," she told him candidly. "And not as in 'summer vacation.' This was where we lived. In the years when we had a little money, or a friend, we'd be in a trailer. Other times, it was a tent."

His faint smile was largely quizzical, as though he couldn't imagine such a thing. "I remember when people used to camp here. It's not allowed anymore. They have to go down by the railroad tracks, to the government campground." He paused, looking at her closely. "I remember the old crowd. But I thought they were mostly gypsies."

She smiled, nodding. "Some were. I knew a lot of gypsies in those days."

He frowned. "You're not a gypsy."

"No. My mother was Hispanic and my father..." Her voice trailed off without finishing the sentence.

"Yes?"

Pushing back the dark hair that the breeze was tossing into her face, she shook her head. "Never mind my father. He never did figure into anything anyway."

A shadow of something that looked close to outrage crept across his face and she stopped, wondering what she'd said that had affected him so strongly and in seconds, the look was gone. He didn't say anything but he came up to join her on the bridge and together they leaned on the railing, looking down into the small, babbling stream.

"Too bad the water doesn't last too well into the summer," he said. "This is actually a pretty little river in the spring."

She nodded. "I remember. Some years the water would last. Flood years, I guess."

Looking around, she tried to remember exactly where she and her mother had pitched their tent that last time when she was thirteen. There was the little stucco bathroom and the meeting room attached. Sometimes the county put on summer craft classes in the meeting room. She'd loved those. For just a moment she heard those childish voices echoing through the trees. It had been fun, like a campout that lasted all summer. Everyone was poor. They were all in the same boat. And there had been so many children, there was always someone to do something with.

"You're smiling," Matt said. "Good memories?"

"Some good, some bad." She looked up at him. "The good ones were mostly when I was young. As I got into the teenage years, the shame of living here began to overwhelm everything else. Then it really wasn't fun anymore."

"What did you come here for?" he asked, turning in order to see her better and hooking his elbows over the railing. "And what did you do the rest of the year?"

She looked up at him. His blue eyes were earnest. He was really interested. Something inside her sang and she smiled.

"Let me tell you this way," she said, suddenly eager to unburden herself of this story. If he really wanted to know who she was, she was going to tell him. "My mother's name was Marina Torres. She was very beautiful when she was young. Her parents were sharecroppers and she wanted to break away from that. She wanted to do things, go places, make something of herself. And her first step was to work as a housekeeper at the ranch of a rich family. It was her big opportunity. They paid well and treated her very well and she thought she was on her way. She was saving her money, planning to go to Dallas and get an education."

"Good for her."

"Yes. Unfortunately there was a handsome young man in the family who was often around. She fell in love." She shrugged grandly, palms out. "And ended up with no job, no lover, no future—only me."

He almost seemed shocked by that. "What happened? Couldn't she get any help from the father?"

She turned to look over the rolling hills of the park. "You know, I'm not even sure if she ever tried. If she did, she never told me about it. She quit her job and went away to hide from the world and to have me. And then she had a young baby to drag around with her everywhere so it was pretty hard to get a good job. From then on, it seemed her life was in a downward spiral. She got odd jobs here and there, a little housekeeping, a little waitressing, and then we'd move on. Once she worked as a dog walker and we lived in a room behind a veterinarians' clinic. I liked that one. All those dogs! But nothing ever lasted very long. We were always moving. Still, most summers, we came back to Chivaree."

"And why was that?"

She hesitated. How was she going to explain that without giving away her secret? "It was largely a community thing, I think," she said at last, and it was mostly true, though it ignored the biggest pull that had started the tradition—her father's presence in the town. "The same people came back here every summer. It was like coming home. Our only safe place in a pretty scary world."

"So coming to Coyote Park is like visiting the scenes of your childhood."

She waved an arm. "It's more than that," she said with sudden bitter insight. "It's déjà vu all over again."

He gazed at her questioningly and she knew she should say something bright and chipper and go back to the car. But she was being honest with Matt. Painfully honest. Why stop now?

"I hated growing up the way I did. I always swore I'd never end up like my mother. I'd do better." Her laugh was hollow. "And look at me now. What a joke. I've ended up just like she did."

Matt moved as though her words exasperated him. Taking her by the shoulders, he forced her to face him. "You haven't ended up as anything," he said evenly. "You're young. You're only just beginning. This is very different from what your mother went through."

There was fire in his eyes that startled her. It seemed odd that he would care so much about this.

"How is it different? I'm doing exactly the same things, making the same mistakes. It almost seems as if I'm fated to relive history." She looked at him, trying to make him understand. "Don't you see? That's why I think it might be best to give this baby to a good couple. I have to do something to break the chain."

"No. You're not going to relive history." He sounded so sure of himself. "You've got someone to help you stay away from that."

She looked up at him, wide eyed. "Who?"

"Me."

She'd known he was going to say that, but she still didn't believe him. "But Matt, who am I to you, really? Why would you do this?"

He stared down at her for a long moment, either unable or unwilling to give her a credible explanation.

"I have my own reasons," he said at last, and then he turned and started walking back toward the car.

She started after him, intent on insisting on a better

answer to her question, but her shoe snagged on a loose board, throwing her off balance, and suddenly she was catapulting forward. Matt turned just in time and caught her.

"Oh!" she cried, looking up at him.

His arms were around her, holding her close, closer than necessary, and she was forced to feel the thick muscles of his arms and his chest.

"You again?" he said with a half smile, looking down at her and shaking his head. "You just can't stop falling for me, can you?"

And then his gaze changed. His eyes clouded with an emotion that made her catch her breath. She was suddenly very much aware of her swollen breasts pressing against him and she knew he was, too. He was going to kiss her. She was sure of it. She should be pushing him away, making sure that didn't happen. But she was frozen right where she was, unable to move. Realization swept through her. She *wanted* him to kiss her.

It was more than craving his protection, more than appreciating his help. There was something between them that sparked and sizzled. There was an excitement, a mystery. And the whole thing needed a kiss to seal it. She lifted her face toward his, her lips slightly parted. She saw the answering flare in his gaze. He wanted her. Despite everything, he wanted her. She could hardly breathe.

And then…it didn't happen. Slowly, he drew back and disentangled her from his embrace. Ostentatiously, he glanced at his watch.

"You know, I've got a meeting to get to," he said,

turning back toward where the car was parked and motioning to indicate that he would follow her.

She moved automatically, walking stiffly. He was saying something the whole time, chatting in a friendly manner, but she didn't hear a word he said. Her face was flushing, her blood was racing. He wasn't going to kiss her after all. She'd laid herself out there like a tray of fine chocolates and he'd turned up his nose. She knew she should be grateful that he'd saved them both from something they'd both vowed to avoid, but she couldn't quite go that far. In fact, deep down, she was furious.

The rest of the afternoon at work dragged slowly. It was pretty hard getting her mind back on filing systems when all she wanted to do was demand an explanation from Matt.

Just tell me why! she kept thinking, but she couldn't say the words out loud.

And deep down, she knew that what she really wanted was much more than an explanation. She wanted that kiss, darn it all!

His meeting didn't last long and he was in his office for the next couple of hours. Every time she looked up, there he was and her heart would give a little lurch. Just because she was upset with him, she quickly reminded herself. Not for anything more serious than that. It was just that her back went up. It had nothing to do with falling for the guy. She wasn't about to do that. No man was going to take control of her destiny again. She was in charge. No one was going to tell her what to do.

Not that he was doing anything overt at the moment. His attitude was completely professional. In fact, it was so cool and distant, she half expected him to start calling her Miss Torres at any moment.

Good. That was just the way it should be. She should be perfectly happy. But there was something about looking into those blue eyes that made her heart do that little stutter thing. She hated that.

She really should go and she knew it. This was all too tempting. At any moment she might find herself giving in to the urge to lean on Matt just a little too much. He offered a safe haven. But she knew that was just the cheese on the trigger to the trap. One touch, and she would be caught for good.

Quitting time finally came and she left him still working at his desk. That gave her the chance to get back to the Allman house before he did, much to her relief. *Anything* to begin to negate the picture of the two of them being a couple. Still, she was a little nervous going in to brave the other Allmans on her own. She wasn't sure what her reception would be.

She parked her car on the street, then took the front walk and knocked on the door. Rita flung it open almost immediately.

"You don't need to knock," she told her as she let her in. "You live here now. Make yourself at home." Turning, she led the way through the front room. "We're all out in the kitchen fixing dinner." She glanced down at the evidence of Annie's pregnancy. "But you must be tired. Why don't you go lie down? We'll call you when it's time to eat."

"I'm not all that tired," Annie protested, wondering just how ragged she must look. She felt as though she'd been running marathons. "I'd like to come out to the kitchen and help."

Rita hesitated. "Oh, okay," she said. "Come on, then."

Jodie was at the counter mixing together a butter-and-garlic concoction to smear on slices of thick sourdough bread she had laid out in a flat pan. Shelley was unpacking a large tray that looked familiar to Annie. They both greeted her warmly.

"I don't know if you've met our little brother David," Rita said, pointing out an extremely handsome, athletic-looking young man draped across a tall bar stool and smiling at her. "As you can see, he was born to be a surfer, but somehow got misplaced in the middle of Texas, far from the ocean."

"Ah, cruel fate," he agreed, coming off the stool to shake hands with Annie. "But I've got my board waxed down just in case there's a good rainstorm."

They all laughed. Annie could tell he was lovable, just by the way the others reacted to him.

"Welcome to the madhouse," he told her. "It's wedding central around here. Don't even try to bring up a topic that doesn't have something to do with matrimony."

"I'm afraid he's got a point," Rita said ruefully. "We're planning a huge wedding, plus a major family prewedding party the week before, and we're all working our fingers to the bone trying to get ready for it all. Half the town is invited to the actual event."

"Well, the Allman half, anyway," Jodie put in. "The McLaughlin half—that's another story."

Shelley, looking a bit stricken, turned to Jodie and took her hand. "I wish it wasn't like that, Jodie. If things were different, we could make it a double wedding."

Jodie nodded, looking wistful, her eyes misting. Impulsively, she hugged her future sister-in-law.

"I would love that, Shelley. But it wouldn't really be fair to Kurt to ask him to have a ceremony that left his family out. And you know no McLaughlins are going to come to a wedding in our yard."

"And we wouldn't go to a wedding in theirs," David reminded them.

"True enough."

Annie felt a pang for all of them. This stupid feud. Then she realized that Jodie's intended was Kurt McLaughlin. His father was Richard McLaughlin, her own father's brother. So that meant Kurt was her cousin.

"Is Kurt coming to dinner?" she asked Jodie, then hoped she hadn't sounded too eager. What would the woman be thinking of her?

"Oh, you haven't met him, have you? Yes, he is coming. You'll love him right away. Everybody does."

David groaned and Jodie swatted at him with a dish towel.

"That'll be another wedding to suffer through," he teased her. "Why do you all scorn the good old-fashioned tradition of eloping? So much easier for everyone."

"I take it you're not married," Annie said, smiling at his tone.

"Nope. I've been spared so far. But it's hardly my turn. After all, Rafe and Jodie just finally committed.

And Matt isn't anywhere near doing the same. So I've got miles to go before I can be pressured about it."

"Why, David," Jodie teased, "you've already about gone through all the women in town. What are you going to do when your supply runs out? Going to move to a new town and start all over?"

He shrugged, leaning back with an attractive devil-may-care attitude. "I'm going to find somebody. It's bound to happen any time now. I'm sort of hankering toward settlin' down, ya know."

Jodie rolled her eyes. "I'll believe that when I see it."

They all laughed and Annie helped Shelley pull the foil off the tray of food she'd brought with her. "Mom sent over this pan of lasagna," Shelley said. "She makes the best in town, doesn't she?"

"Oh, yes," Annie agreed. "One of my favorites." If there was one thing Millie knew how to do it was to cook up some great food.

She looked around for something else to help with. Jodie was working on the garlic bread, Shelley on the lasagna and Rita was cutting up greens for salad.

"Shall I set the table?" Annie asked.

"Sure, if you want to." Rita wiped her hands and reached into a cupboard. "Here are the mats and some plastic cutlery. I think we'll eat outside on the picnic table so we don't have to move all the wedding supplies on the dining room table."

Annie took the utensils and mats and headed out the back door and into the backyard. The area included a small vegetable garden alongside the house and a large green lawn that led down into a canyon rimmed with pine and cottonwood. A couple of gardeners were busy clearing sections along the perimeter and planting beds of annuals, probably in preparation for the wedding. In a few weeks, the yard would be crowded with people celebrating an Allman marriage.

Annie smiled despite the pang she felt. Would she ever have her own wedding? Did she even want one? She put a hand on her belly and felt a sudden connection to the baby within, a connection stronger than she'd ever felt before. And along with it came a feeling of well-being that calmed her.

"We're going to be okay," she whispered, as much to herself as to the baby. "Whatever happens, we'll make it."

Turning back to the task at hand, she set the long wooden picnic table, making tents of the napkins at each place. She was just standing back to admire her own handiwork when she heard footsteps coming her way. Whirling, she found Matt bearing down on her, looking incredibly handsome with his shirt open at the neck.

"Hi," he said simply.

"Hi yourself," she said back.

For just a moment, there didn't seem to be anything else to say. They stared at each other, both acutely aware of what had happened at the park. Then Annie cleared her throat and spoke.

"I've been thinking things over." She turned from him and looked out on the kitchen garden. "You know, I do appreciate so much you giving me this job and I really do want it. But as far as living here in your house..." She took a deep breath and tried again. "I just don't think I'd better stay."

Chapter Seven

Matt's gaze went hard as flint and almost as cold. "What are you talking about?"

"I can't be here." Shaking her head, she turned to look at him, as though her eyes might be able to convey her meaning if her words couldn't. "Don't you see? It's already the talk of the town. And your family is looking at me cross-eyed. Everyone I see is giving me that 'uh-huh' look as though they think they know what's *really* going on. And I just can't take it."

He was still looking at her darkly, but he nodded slowly at the same time. He knew what she was talking about and, reluctantly, he was acknowledging it. "You think it would be best if we weren't together quite so much," he noted. "And I've got to admit, you're probably right."

Their eyes met. He didn't have to say anything further. They both knew that the pull between them was getting stronger by the minute. If they didn't do something to head it off, fireworks were on the horizon.

She'd been embarrassed at first for having let him see so clearly that she wanted his kiss on the bridge that afternoon, and then not getting it. But her embarrassment had faded. She could tell that he understood. He knew she'd had a weak moment. Luckily he'd had a strong moment at the same time. They could depend on that, or they could stay away from each other as much as possible. And if that didn't work, maybe she would just head on back to Houston. She had friends there. It wouldn't be the end of the world.

"Don't worry," he said. "I've got the solution."

She sighed and looked up at him sadly. "So do I. I think I'd better move out."

"No, not you," he said calmly. "Me. I'm moving out."

She blinked, not sure for a second if she'd heard him right. "What?"

"It's not a big deal. I'll go stay at Rafe's apartment with him. He's got plenty of room."

Her jaw dropped. "Oh, that's crazy."

"No, it'll be much better for everyone." Now that he'd come to the decision, he seemed almost cheery about it. "All you women can take over the house and dedicate it to wedding preparations and we men will stay out of the way."

"I agree."

Annie whirled to find Rita on the back porch starting down the steps toward them with a tray full of drinks. She seemed to have heard most of their conversation.

"Matt's absolutely right. It would be for the best. We could really use you here as an extra pair of hands, Annie. You have no idea how many table favors and paper roses we're going to be putting together."

"I'll help any way I can," she assured Rita. "But I don't have to stay here to do that."

The older woman put down her tray on the table, took up Annie's hands and held them tightly as she smiled into her eyes.

"Please stay. We do want you to. I'm sorry I overreacted this morning. It was just such a surprise." She flashed a quick look at her brother, a look that seemed to have an apology in it, then refocused on Annie. "The more we get to know you, the more we're glad to have you here."

Annie hesitated. When it came right down to it, she didn't have a lot of good options. And the way the invitation was being presented, she could hardly turn it down.

"Well, I suppose we could try it for a while," she said.

Matt nodded, looking perfectly satisfied with the plans as they stood. "By the way, most of the things from your apartment are here. I had the men put all your clothes in your room. The other items are in a storeroom out behind the garage."

"Oh. Thanks so much." It was a relief not to have to go back to that place. Matt did have a way of taking care of things before she even realized that something needed to be done.

She smiled at him. "I guess that settles it. I'll have to stay for the time being."

"Good." He reached up and began to unbutton his shirt as he turned away. "And now that our living plans are taken care of, I'm going to go change into something more comfortable and get ready for dinner."

Funny how just watching him begin to undress caused a strange little flutter in her chest and made her mouth go dry. She smiled at Rita nervously, hoping it wasn't obvious, and began to help her put out the drinks at the places she'd set. It looked like she was going to stay, but she couldn't keep a sense of disquiet completely hidden inside. It would be better if she was on her own, away from the temptations Matt offered and the trap of depending on others. She knew from experience that help like that could evaporate on you just when you needed it most. She was going to have to stay strong. No doubt about it.

Dinner was lively and fun. Everyone talked and Annie hardly got a word in but she felt as if she got to know them all very quickly. Meeting Kurt was a highlight. Tall and handsome, he had a friendly smile and an easy way about him.

And…he was her cousin! It was so amazing to have all these relatives, even if the relationship was one-sided. And she could tell she was going to like Kurt as much as she liked Josh. She watched as his gaze followed Jodie whenever she moved more than a few feet away from him. He was totally in love with her. And he was obviously such a good guy. Didn't that show the rest of them that McLaughlins might be human, too?

Turning, she found Matt's gaze trained on her just as firmly and she flushed. She wanted to tell him to cut it out, that the others would notice. But she had to admit, it warmed a little hidden place in her heart.

"I'm going to run up to see Jesse," Kurt said as they began to clear the dishes away. "I've got some things to report to him."

Annie grimaced. She hadn't seen Jesse Allman yet. He wasn't well and seemed to spend all his time in bed up in his room at the top of the house. It was a little scary thinking of him up there, like a spider weaving plots. She shivered, not sure why she'd conjured up that picture. It was probably based on her childhood fear of the man and was totally unfair. Maybe.

A half hour later the dishes were done and the others were getting out a board game to play, but Annie had noticed Matt slip away some time before and he hadn't come back yet. She found herself making excuses and following him upstairs. They did have a few more things that needed to be dealt with. Maybe he would have time for a little talk.

Matt heard someone coming down the hall and he wondered if it would be Annie. He'd left his door ajar and was making enough noise while packing his suitcase to lead anyone toward his location. Had he done that on purpose, to make sure she would find her way to him? What the hell? Why not?

And then, there she was, looking in on him, her mass of curly dark hair flying around her face, one strand falling over her eyes in a deliciously seductive way that made his gut churn.

"What are you doing?" she asked, looking as though she were stricken with guilt.

"I'm packing." He threw a couple of socks in, then

glanced at her again, but kept on working. And he couldn't help but notice how her arrival seemed to brighten the room.

That was just the problem. She'd changed his life. Yes, ridiculous as it was, a woman he barely knew had thrown his sense of comfortable stability for a loop. In fact, she'd taken over his mind. When she'd fallen into his life, he'd been preoccupied with finding his baby, wandering around like a man possessed, calling the private detective he'd hired five times a day to check on progress. Now he was preoccupied with Annie as well. All this preoccupation was crowding out anything close to a normal life. In other words, he couldn't get her out of his head. And didn't really want to.

"I feel so bad about kicking you out of your own house," she was saying, standing at a distance, but close enough for him to feel the effect of her presence acutely.

"You're not kicking me out of anything. I'm glad to escape from this pressurized atmosphere."

"The wedding madness?"

"Exactly." And a lot more.

Annie, Annie, if you only knew how you put a guy on edge just hearing your voice. And catching your scent in the air. And getting a glimpse of your pretty face, looking so concerned.

His body was responding. This was crazy. He felt as if he were on something. Overcaffeinated. Overstimulated. Over the top.

Oh, hell. I've got to get out of here.

She sat down on the bed and gave a bounce. It was a good bed, firm but with a nice spring to it. She bounced again, looking delighted, like a child on a carnival ride. He almost groaned aloud. Not only was she outrageously adorable, the bouncing was bringing to mind how good she would feel in his arms, how they would move together, how the mattress would give, then harden under them… Oh, lord, the woman had no mercy.

But then, hopefully she didn't understand how crazy he was getting to be about her. What on earth had caused him to fall for a woman who was about to have a baby that wasn't his? Penny—wasn't that it? And his guilt over not being there for her when she needed him? That was how it started, but this was going way too far. He kept telling himself it was just a passing thing, a momentary madness, and that it would fade away very soon. His sanity would return to him. Someday he would look back on these days with mild amusement, wondering what had caused him to go nuts for a while.

Oh, yeah. Dream on.

"Is this the same room you've had since you were a little boy?" she asked him.

"Nope. This part of the house was added when I was in high school. But I've had this room ever since then. It's been my base, my anchor. I went away to college and came back to this room. Same with medical school."

She nodded, looking about at the photographs of his mother and various friends, the baseball trophies, the books and magazines. He felt a twinge of remorse for talking about how important his room was to him as he remembered what she'd told him at the park, about how she'd grown up without a place to call her own. Along with everything else, he had a strong protective urge toward her. He didn't want anything hurting her. But he knew in his heart that he himself was the most likely to do that.

Yes, moving out was the best answer to the problem.

Sliding off the bed, she started surveying the titles in his bookcase. "I thought maybe we ought to go over a few things," she said without looking around. "I'd better warn you that I'm going to have to take an hour off next Friday morning. I've got a checkup with Dr. Marin."

Raising his head, he looked at her speculatively. "You know, I could—"

"No, you couldn't." Glancing over her shoulder at him, she shuddered delicately. "What do you think—that you're going to come in and deliver the baby when the time comes?"

His grin was lopsided. The prospect actually charmed him. "I could if I had to."

"No way."

She was right, of course. He was getting too close to her to be objective. Dr. Marin was a good doctor, he supposed. He was going to have to trust him with her.

"And, of course, there's Thursdays. I need those afternoons off."

"Yes, I know. You said that before."

That again. He'd been hoping she would get over her sense that she needed to keep that extra job. He was going to control his annoyance. That much he had promised himself. But she had to understand how impossible it was for her to work for the McLaughlins.

"We need to talk about that."

She turned and gazed right at him. "There's nothing

to talk about. I work at the McLaughlin Ranch on Thursday afternoons."

Anger Management 101 said to count to ten before speaking. He only got to five. "Well, you're going to have to stop that," he said firmly.

"No," she replied just as firmly if not more so. Her eyes flashed. "That's one thing I won't stop."

Her tone and manner brought him up short. She really meant it. He found it hard to believe that she would throw away everything just to keep a part-time job out at McLaughlin Ranch.

"I really don't want you to do this," he said as calmly as he could.

She didn't waver. "I'm sorry about that. But I'm going to do it. Nothing you say will stop me."

He shook his head, mystified. "What's so special about this job?"

"It's not the job. It's Josh and Cathy McLaughlin. I enjoy working for them."

"Okay, then what's so special about them?"

She caught her breath, hesitating, then said, "They need me. And I like them."

It was more than that. He knew instinctively that something was going on here. But he also knew that she wasn't likely to come clean about it if he pushed her too hard. So he tried a little sideways action. Sitting down on the edge of the bed, he leaned back against the headboard, watching her through narrowed eyes.

"What exactly do you do there?" he asked her.

She looked at him, then gingerly sat down at the foot of the bed herself.

"Well, I call it housekeeping, but it's actually more like baby-sitting with a little cleaning and food preparation thrown in." She looked to see if he was listening. "I go every Thursday afternoon for four hours. That gives Cathy some time to go shopping by herself or to meet some friends for lunch or go to the dentist. She really needs that time off. She spends most of every day working on that ranch with the baby practically strapped to her back."

He frowned thoughtfully. "From what I've heard, Josh is actually doing a pretty good job of bringing the ranch back to being a going concern after his father darn near ran it into the ground. But I'm sure it's a big project."

Annie stole a look at his face. What he was saying was what she'd surmised but hadn't heard put quite that clearly before.

"How did you get to know them?" he asked.

"I saw the job advertised and I applied for it."

"You didn't know them before?"

"No."

He was quiet for a moment, and she waited, letting him absorb the information.

"You do know about the feud, don't you?" he asked her at last.

"Of course. No one can grow up in Chivaree, even part-time, and not know about the feud. It started about the time the town was founded, didn't it?"

He nodded.

"That's a long time." She raised an eyebrow archly. "Don't you think it's about time to end it?"

"End it?" The concept was a surprise to him, as though she'd suggested breathing water instead of air. "You can't end something that old."

She rolled her eyes. "You know, this silly feud may be important to the Allmans and it may be important to the McLaughlins, but to the rest of us, outside your paranoid little world, it means absolutely nothing. I think you should all grow up and get over it."

"Easy for you to say," he muttered, but his mind had moved on to something else. She'd mentioned her checkup with Dr. Marin and now he remembered she'd said something about his being involved in her adoption plans. "Is Dr. Marin your liaison with the adoption lawyer?" he asked.

She turned to look at him, wary surprise in her eyes. "Yes."

He grimaced, raking his fingers through his hair. "You know, you've got other options. We should talk about—"

"It's a good option," she said evenly. She didn't wait to hear what his ideas might be. "Adoptions can work. There are many wonderful instances of adoption going so well. Just look at—" She was about to say Josh and Cathy, but she stopped in time. He didn't want to hear about McLaughlin adoptions, she was sure.

"I know that," he responded with a touch of impatience. "I just want you to be sure you know what you're doing, that you've looked at every alternative."

He could tell she was biting her tongue to keep from snapping at him. "Matt, do you really think I'm going into this on a whim? Of course I've thought about it, long and hard."

He frowned, then shook his head. "Annie, just because your mother's experience was not so hot doesn't mean that you will have the same life. Things have loosened up a lot since then. You're smart, you're educated, you'll have opportunities she couldn't have dreamed of."

"You don't know anything about it. I lived it. I have to think of the future for this baby. A child does best in a two-parent home." She looked at him defiantly. "You don't think a child needs both a mother and a father?" she challenged.

"Oh, absolutely. If possible. That's why..." His words trailed off and he took a deep breath.

His tone drew her attention and when she looked into his eyes, they were stormy in a way that sent up warning signals all through her system.

"I've got something I should tell you about, Annie," he said softly. "I should have told you about this before, but it's a hard thing to tell. It isn't going to make you think any better of me."

"Why? What is it?"

The sound of laughter filled the air. A few of the others were coming up the stairs. Matt grabbed her hand.

"We can't really talk here. I'll go out and head them off, then you go down the back way to the backyard. I'll meet you out there."

She rose from the bed, looking at him with a worried frown between her beautiful eyebrows, and then she stood back to let him go. But just as he passed her, she reached out and touched his arm, as though to comfort him. As though she could read his mind and knew what was bothering him. He paused, looking down into her pretty face for a moment, then moved on toward the others. But that simple gesture spoke volumes. How could he keep from falling for this woman when she kept doing things like that?

Annie waited in the shadows of an old pecan tree that stood like a sentinel along the margins of the backyard. There was a light on in the window at the top of the house and she knew that had to be where Jesse Allman was. A place where she didn't want to go.

Matt came out the back door and she moved forward to meet him. She had no idea what he was going to tell her but she assumed it probably had something to do with the pained, brooding look that often came over his face. She hadn't known what to attribute it to. Now, maybe she would find out.

"Hi," she said, as though they hadn't just parted company moments earlier.

"Thanks for coming out here," he told her. "Let's walk down by the edge of the canyon."

"Okay."

There were lights strung up in the trees around the yard but the lighting wasn't perfect and he took her hand to steady her as they walked across the grass. His touch was warm. She tried to ignore it. Their steps slowed as they reached the edge of the dark canyon and he dropped her hand. The sound of water rushing over rocks at the bottom of the canyon made a background of sound. The evening air was cool. Annie turned to look at Matt, but she had a hard time making out his features in the dim light.

"This isn't a big secret," he told her, as though he were afraid she might have taken the wrong idea from his earlier words. "Everyone else in the house already knows about it. It's just that I hadn't told you yet, and I thought you ought to know."

She smiled at him encouragingly. "Then I guess you'd better tell me."

He took a deep breath and began. "You know the part your father played in your life? The thing you seem to despise him for?" He shoved his hands into the pockets of his slacks. "Well, I've done the same thing he did. I've got a baby out there that I don't know."

A shock ran through her. "Oh, Matt."

He looked out over the canyon. "I only found out about it a couple of months ago."

Even in the dark, she could see his tortured expression. Reaching out, she put a hand on his upper arm. "What happened?" she asked softly.

He hesitated, looking down at her. "Okay, let me start from the beginning. I went to medical school in Dallas, then did my internship and residency there, too. For a period of a few months I had a relationship with a woman named Penny. She was a lot of fun and we had a great time together." He looked away again. "Eventually, we had a physical relationship. Then things began to come between us and we had a falling out. She left town and I never heard from her again."

Annie nodded. She understood that sort of thing. Happened every day and seemed so harmless at the time. But the ramifications were often huge, like the pebble in the pond. "Were you in love?"

"Love?" He looked surprised that she would even bring it up. "It was a very casual relationship. We were both young and I don't think either of us considered it true love."

She nodded again, yet she couldn't help but wonder if Penny had felt the same way Matt had. After all, it was different if you were the one who was going to carry the baby—a fact she knew only too well.

"Anyway, a few weeks ago I got a call from an old friend who had known us both and in the course of conversation, he asked how Penny was. I told him I didn't know and he asked what had ever happened to our baby." He winced even now, thinking of that conversation and how it had hit him. "I was stunned."

"You had no idea."

"No."

"Have you tried to find Penny?"

"Yes. It was Shelley, actually, who found Penny's brother living in San Antonio. I brought him here to Chivaree and got him a job at Allman Industries." He paused and grimaced before he went on. "But tragically, Penny had died. And no one knows whatever happened to the baby."

"Oh, my gosh!" Her hands went to her mouth. That was a twist she hadn't expected.

Turning, he reached out to lean against a low tree limb. "I've hired a private investigator, but so far, no leads."

"Oh, Matt, I'm so sorry."

Leaning his back against the tree, he looked at her. "So you see, that gives me a different perspective on your situation and your plan to give your baby up for adoption. I'm afraid my baby was adopted. I may never find him…or her."

That put a lump in her throat. She felt sorry for him, sorry for Penny, sorry for the baby who was who-knew-where. She moved closer. "But Matt, I think it's a credit to you that you are trying."

He snorted softly. "A little late."

"My father never tried at all," she mused, more to herself than to him. "Of course, I'm not sure he even knew about me. It's possible he didn't."

He looked away. "I keep wondering if she tried to tell me, if I was just insensitive and ignored the signs. I'm a medical professional for God's sake. I should have seen the evidence."

She put her hand on his arm again, wishing she knew what she could do to comfort him. "Matt, don't do that to yourself. For all you know, *she* didn't know until after she left you."

He looked down at her face upturned toward his with such an earnest look and his own relaxed into a faint smile. "Annie…" He touched her cheek with his fore-finger. "Do you despise me now?"

"Oh, Matt! I could never, never…" Words weren't enough. Somehow she had to show him.

When she threw her arms around his neck and pressed herself to him, she hadn't really meant for it to end in a kiss. At least, she didn't think that was what she'd meant to do. Still, it happened. One second she was murmuring reassurance and comfort and the next, she was spellbound.

That was the only way she could describe it when she thought about it later—and she thought about it a lot. It wasn't as though she was a novice in the kissing department. She'd had boyfriends over the years, and of course, there had been Rick. Even as a teenager, there had been experiments during stolen moments at Coyote Park, among other places. She liked kissing. With the right sort of men.

And Matt was all wrong. She knew that, had hoped to hold back what that did to her. When he'd kissed her the night before, it had been fleeting, casual, almost friendly, and he'd pulled back and apologized. But this was different. No apologies were going to cancel out this kiss.

His mouth was hot on hers, hot and hungry, and she responded immediately, just as urgently, her tongue sliding against his, her body arching to feel as much of him against her as she could get. His hands slid up under her shirt, fingers just rough enough to tantalize her smooth skin. And the spell took hold.

She'd stepped off the edge of reality and was spinning in a new place where her mind shut down and her senses took over. Small things took on a huge new importance—the minty scent of his aftershave, the sultry taste of his skin, the sweet torture of the touch of his palm as it cupped her breast. She moaned with pleasure, grinding against him, and his kisses traveled down the chord of her neck, almost biting, but not quite, sending her into a special sort of ecstasy. She wanted him in a way she'd never wanted a man before. How could that be? It was all wrong. And yet, it had never felt so right.

When she finally found the strength to pull back, she was gasping for breath, and his breathing was just as ragged. Looking down at her, he framed her face with his hands, his intense gaze searching her eyes, and he half laughed.

"Oh, Annie, I can't believe how much I want you." He spoke softly but his words tore out of him as though it was agony for him to admit it.

"Which is exactly why we can't do this again," she noted breathlessly. But she said it so sadly, he laughed again, pulling her close and holding her for a moment, her head against his chest.

"Okay," he said, releasing her at last with obvious regret. "We'll be good."

"We'll be good," she echoed ruefully. "Or die trying."

They strolled back toward the house, talking quietly, her hand in his. But he'd dropped it by the time they reached the others, and he rather gruffly said his goodbyes, grabbed his suitcase and left. Afterward, Annie went to her own room to give herself some time to savor that kiss. Savor it, and vow it wouldn't happen again.

Thursday afternoon found Annie at the photographer's, helping Cathy get portraits made of baby Emily. She watched Cathy making faces at her child, trying to get her to smile for the camera. And it worked. Suddenly Emily gurgled with baby laughter and the photographer began clicking away.

"Oh, those are going to be so good," Annie said.

"They better be," Cathy responded, sprawling in the

chair beside her, exhausted. "I feel like I've just broken a bronco here. That was hard work!"

By now, Emily's laughter had dissolved into tears and Annie sprang up to get her. She comforted the child while Cathy dealt with the desk, and soon they were back in Cathy's SUV, bouncing along the rutted road to the McLaughlin Ranch.

Annie felt almost as tired as Cathy did. The last few days had been rewarding but they surely had tried her stamina. Working at Allman Industries was turning out well. She had no qualms about the job, only the fact that she had to do it within twenty feet of Matt. It was very hard keeping her mind on her work when the man who made her dizzy was just steps away. So close she could almost hear him breathing.

He'd been acting the perfect gentleman, she had to say. There had been no more kisses. He hadn't even come over to the house since that night. And at the office he'd treated her with a dignified reserve. But that didn't do anything to stifle the way her heart raced whenever she looked at him.

And it was crazy. She knew that very well. Once burned, twice shy, they said. *Hah. Just tell that to my traitorous heart.*

Luckily, she had a reminder to them both. The baby she carried was getting bigger every day. Every time she was tempted to forget all common sense and throw herself at Matt's handsome head, the baby kicked or moved in that adorable way it had, and she remembered. Next week she would see Dr. Marin and he would want to know if she planned to go the adoption route or not. A hard decision, one she would just as soon put off for a while longer.

She looked back at Emily, now sound asleep in her car seat. Matt's words on the subject of adoption came back to her. She couldn't deny that his arguments had shaken some of her own opinions on whether or not she should go through with it. Glancing at Cathy in the driver's seat, she had a thought. Maybe she could use some input from the other side of the equation.

"Cathy, tell me about Emily. How you adopted her."

Cathy threw her a quick smile. "We found her in San Antonio. It was a private adoption, through a lawyer. Someone who had worked for the McLaughlins for years."

"You were lucky."

"Yes."

"I've heard adoptions are much more difficult nowadays."

"Sometimes they are. It depends on the circumstances." Cathy gave her a sideways look. "Actually, we ended up having the paperwork handled over the border in order to avoid a few rules that might have held us up for months. The lawyer is a real expert in these things and he took care of everything."

"Do you know much about her birth mother?"

Cathy shook her head. "Not a thing. We have some medical information in case it ever becomes necessary. But that's all." She glanced back and smiled at her darling child. "Actually, when we adopted her, the lawyer said that Emily's birth mother requested someone from Chivaree. Something about it all coming full circle.

Which makes me think she must have been from Chivaree herself. I didn't question anything at the time. Once I took one look at her, I just wanted my baby in my arms. But I sometimes look around at girls walking by when I'm downtown and wonder, could it be her?"

"I guess you'll never know."

"And I hope she doesn't know anything about us. You read about these nightmare situations where birth parents try to get their babies back years later. Every time I think of such a thing, my heart stops. It's kind of a strange position to be in and yet, it doesn't really matter. Emily is so ours. She couldn't be more my baby if I'd had twelve hours of screaming labor to get her."

Annie smiled. "I know. I've seen it."

If only Matt could see how this little family created such a warm, loving circle she was sure it would change his mind about adoption. Cathy and Josh had made no bones from the beginning about the fact that Emily was adopted. But just looking in from the outside, no one could have guessed it. The bond among them all couldn't have been stronger.

She loved coming to their house and seeing them interact. Sometimes she felt guilty for taking money for being there. She would have gladly come without that. In no time at all, Cathy and Josh had become among the very closest friends she'd ever had. Her heart ached to think that the relationship they had might be shattered when the facts came out. There was no easy way to break it to Josh that his father was her father, too.

Maybe she should have been truthful right from the start. But if she had, would they have let her into their lives this way? Would she have experienced this? Unfortunately there were no easy answers. All she knew for sure was that she didn't want to hurt anyone unnecessarily. And maybe, in order to do that, she should withdraw without telling them anything at all…

Cathy pulled the car to a stop at a red light and turned to look at her. "Why all these questions, Annie? Are you thinking about putting your baby up for adoption?"

Annie hesitated. She wasn't as brave about it anymore. "I don't know. It's an option I'm considering."

"It's a heartbreaking decision to make, I know," Cathy said. "And no one can make it but you." Reaching out, she took Annie's hand. "Please know Josh and I will be there for you whatever you decide."

Annie felt tears threatening. What the heck was this? She was turning into a waterfall. It had to be the pregnancy. Hormones. Whatever, it was darn annoying.

But she also felt tremendous gratitude to Cathy. She knew things might be very different once the truth was out. All promises would be off by then. Still, it was nice to know they felt this way for the moment.

Josh was in the kitchen as they came into the house. He rose without his usual smile as he faced them.

"Annie," he said, looking troubled. "What's this about you living with the Allmans?"

Chapter Eight

Annie gasped softly, then hoped Josh hadn't noticed. She should have told him and Cathy about this when she first arrived today. It was too late to remedy that now, but she would do her best to smooth that over with a few facts. She explained quickly about what had happened, about the fainting at Millie's, about Matt's concern for her pregnancy and him showing up at her apartment in the middle of the night when chaos was happening next door.

"So he just sort of took you in?" Cathy asked, looking intrigued.

She nodded.

"Well, that seems mighty neighborly of him." Josh's voice was edgy with sarcasm, causing Cathy to give him a reproving glance.

"It was because of my pregnancy I think. He…has reasons to feel especially interested in new babies right now." She hesitated and then decided not to explain how he felt about adoption.

"So is he the first Allman you've ever met?" Josh asked her, scooping Emily up in his arms and looking a little more relaxed as his baby girl laughed and tried to grab his ears.

Annie grinned at him as he fended Emily off. "He was my first. Now I know tons of them."

"We'd better introduce you to some of our McLaughlin relatives fast to provide a sort of antidote," Josh said, only half teasing as he set Emily down again, watching as she ran off to play in her own room. "Too much time with the Allmans has been known to drive the innocent to madness."

"I guess I'm not all that innocent," Annie retorted.

His gaze sharpened. "You do know about the feud between our two families?"

"Oh, yes. I've heard about it for years." Walking toward the pantry, Annie began putting away some of the groceries they had picked up at the store on the way home. "It's pretty much ancient history, though, wouldn't you say? Isn't it time to bury the hatchet?"

He followed her, thumbs hooked in the belt loops of his jeans. "Funny thing about a feud like that. It becomes part of the air you breathe. It becomes ingrained in your heritage. It's a part of you, even though most of us don't remember what started it all."

"What do you suppose did start it?" Cathy asked. She wasn't originally from Chivaree so much of this story was new to her, too, Annie noted.

"Well, the two families were the founders of the

town. That often sets up an adversarial relationship just on the face of it. And I think there was a lot of rustlin' of horses and stealing of each other's women and things like that going on in the old days. That was generations ago, of course."

"So why is the feud still going on now?" Annie asked, folding the brown paper bag.

"I don't know. Growing up it just becomes a part of you. And then you go to school and everyone expects you to stick to your own side and they egg you on. It just continues. The teenaged years are the worst, I guess. We McLaughlins were always pitted against the Allmans at everything. Especially the years where the rodeo thing was big. We were always trying to outride or outbust one or another of them. That's just the way it is."

"How does Kurt avoid it?" she asked.

"So you've met Kurt?" A smile lit his eyes for a moment. "Good old Kurt. Funny, I used to like him best out of all my cousins, and now he's turned traitor and gone and joined up with other side."

She turned on him, frowning. "See, when you put it that way, it sounds bad. But maybe Kurt could be a bridge."

"A bridge?" He made a face. "Who needs a bridge? Who wants a bridge between the Allmans and the McLaughlins?"

But she sort of liked the idea. "Maybe *I* could be a bridge," she murmured, and then looked up quickly when she realized she'd said it out loud.

He was looking at her curiously, obviously wondering why she would say such a thing. She flushed and realized it was time to be getting home.

But she wavered. Here it was, her big opportunity. The conversation had set it up perfectly. The time was ripe. She could tell them right now. Right this minute. She bit her lip, trying to make herself do it.

But she realized that she didn't have the nerve. Not yet, anyway.

"So tell me," she said instead, facing Josh. "I'm going to be living with the Allmans for another few weeks at least. Is this going to be a problem?"

He looked at her for a long moment, then he smiled. "No, of course not," he said.

Cathy breathed a sigh of relief. "Thank goodness. My husband is sane after all."

Annie smiled but she thought she understood Josh a little better than Cathy did. The feud would always be there. Bridge or no bridge, it wasn't going away. There was just no getting around that one.

If Annie had thought the tension would relax when Matt moved in with his brother and wasn't around to provoke her all the time at the house, she might as well have saved herself the trouble. That theory was proved wrong right away. Even in the office, there was electricity between the two of them that she couldn't deny.

That doesn't mean you have to act on it, she kept telling herself incessantly. *In fact, you can't. And you won't. And he won't, either.*

She would be working on a knotty problem, her face twisted with the intensity of her concentration, and then something would compel her to look up and across the office—and there he was at his own desk, staring at her with a look on his face that she couldn't quite interpret. And some little devil of delicious shivering would start up inside her.

Other times it was just the sense of his presence in the room. She could feel him even when she didn't turn and look at him. It wasn't that he was staring at her or anything like that. He was just there. And something about him filled her consciousness with pleasure at the oddest times.

She was getting the office arranged in ways that seemed to amaze him. Maybe it was her nursing experience that helped her know how medical matters should be systematized. Maybe it was the natural inborn ability to organize. At any rate, the office was running more smoothly than it ever had.

Matt was already involved in operating a vaccination clinic for employees and she made the calls and set up appointments so that the whole plant was up-to-date by the end of her second week. Then she arranged a lecture series on workplace accidents and contacted a San Antonio firm that would come to give a talk in the future on identity codes for employees' children, including fingerprinting and imbedded microchips.

In the meantime, Matt saw any workplace injuries or illnesses there in his office and also spent part of every day at his private practice—giving Annie a sometimes welcome break from the intensity of his presence. And of course, there was the business of Allman Industries to run. Rafe was the acting executive officer, though everyone made sure she knew Jesse Allman wanted Matt to take over the job and clearly he felt pressured to do as his father asked. She would have thought that would make things awkward between him and his brother, but it didn't seem to. Perhaps that was because Matt made no secret of the fact that he wanted to pursue medicine, so there was really little reason for Rafe to feel threatened.

The days went by quickly, so full of work for both of them that there wasn't much time to dwell on the way they felt about each other. When Annie wasn't at work, she was at the Allman house, working on wedding invitations or favors or finger food. It was only late at night that she lay in the soft, heavenly bed and thought about Matt.

Why Matt? She had a sort of crush on the man, she supposed. He had a knack for setting off certain reactions in her, different from any man she'd ever known before. And he'd been more than decent to her. She owed him for that. But once the baby was born and she was on her own two feet again... Yes, then what?

If things were only different, then she would have more scope for dreaming. If she weren't pregnant with another man's baby...if she weren't a McLaughlin...if he weren't an Allman. And then again, if he hadn't just found out about his own baby, he probably wouldn't have given her a second look that day at Millie's. He'd never made that a secret. His interest in her came from the baby she carried. Once that was over, for all she knew, he might not have time for her anymore. Never again was she going to take a man's interest as evidence of deep feeling. Things just didn't work that way.

And dreaming was for people who had the time and luxury for it. She'd had dreams before and look what had come of them. She had other things to think about—like what she was going to do about this baby.

On the day of her appointment with Dr. Marin, she left the office before lunch and waved goodbye to Matt, who scowled at her instead of waving back. The regular checkup didn't take long, but as the doctor was setting up the monitoring equipment, she blurted out something she hadn't even known she was going to say.

"Can you tell me the gender of my baby today?" she asked.

"Of course," he answered. "I'll show you the latest ultrasound I had the technician take last time you were here."

Her heart beat hard with excitement as she realized what she'd requested. She was going to see a picture of her baby. This pregnancy was finally becoming real to her. She wasn't sure that was a good thing.

"You've got a bouncing baby boy in there," Dr. Marin told her with a grin. "All the signs point to the fact that he looks darn healthy, too."

"Oh." She couldn't think of a thing to say. She closed her eyes for a moment of silent prayer, then opened them and felt as though happiness was flowing in her veins.

His grin faded and a small frown took its place. "Have you been thinking about our talk?" he asked. "Was there anything else you wanted to know about the adoption process?"

"No," she said, losing some of the excitement and avoiding his gaze. "I—I still have to think about it."

"No problem," he told her. "But it would be best to

make sure you're in the proper mind-set if you're going to go through with it."

"I'll let you know," she said quickly. "Later."

"Of course."

She left soon after and headed back to work feeling a little shaky. Her baby was due in less than two months. When she'd planned out her trip to Chivaree, she'd told herself to keep her distance from the life growing inside her. She would do her best for the child with proper nutrition and checkup and everything a baby needed to come into the world whole and healthy. But she wouldn't ask to know the gender. She wouldn't let them show her the pictures. She wouldn't think of names. And now she'd taken two steps she hadn't planned to take. If she thought of a name for her baby, she would be taking a third.

"Three strikes and you're out," she whispered to herself as she drove into the parking lot. "No thinking about a name!"

But she knew she was grasping at straws. Patting her rounded belly, she smiled. Her baby was in there, doing great. What could be more wonderful?

Matt didn't ask her how the appointment had gone and was obviously in a foul mood. Glowering and gloomy, he almost bit her head off for the smallest infractions and left for his private practice as soon as he could get away. She breathed a sigh of relief as he went out the door.

To her surprise, he showed up at the house for dinner that night, for the first time since he'd moved out. Still grumpy, he didn't say much. But the others were so full of good spirits, his brooding went largely unnoticed. Kurt had brought along Katy, his year-old child from his first marriage and she was charming everyone. Watching her play to the audience, Annie wondered what her own baby would be like. Would she get to know?

Suddenly she knew she wanted to—very badly. Glancing at Matt, she noted that he was paying no attention. His mind was on something else and he barely noticed the others at all.

But once the dishes had been cleared, he caught Annie alone and stopped her from going back to the dining room where Rita and Jodie were working on decorations.

"Want to go for a walk?" he asked her.

"Where?" she responded, surprised.

"Down the path along the canyon." He indicated the direction with a jerk of his head.

She hesitated, the blood beginning to beat a rhythm in her veins. "Why?"

He gave her a look she could only categorize as exasperation and took her hand, tugging her toward the door. "Come on," he said gruffly.

She let him lead her outside. It was already getting dark and lights twinkled in the trees. They walked toward the canyon but she was getting more and more nervous about this.

"Did you have something you wanted to say to me?" she asked, hoping to speed things up so that they could go back more quickly.

He swung around so that he could look at her, jamming his hands into his pockets. "I'm sorry I've been so annoying to be around today," he told her. "I heard from Dan Kramer, the private investigator looking for my baby this morning."

"Oh! Bad news?"

He hesitated. "Well, not good news. He's about exhausted the leads on records here in Texas. He's afraid the adoption paperwork might have been filed out of state, in which case, it's going to take a small miracle to find it."

"Oh, Matt, I'm sorry." She reached out to touch his arm. "That's rotten. But you shouldn't lose hope. I'm sure he'll find something."

"Maybe. Maybe not. It depends on how accurate the names used in the filing were." He put his hand over hers. "But that's not your problem."

She felt a jolt as his fingers wrapped around hers. His shoulders seemed wide as the horizon and she felt an odd impulse to curl herself into his embrace. She had to fight off that sort of thing. "Sure it is," she said a bit breathlessly. "I care about you."

"Do you?" He looked completely unconvinced. Then he sighed and shook his head as though he was fed up with himself as well as everything else. "Oh, hell, Annie. I just want to be with you. I want to talk to you and look at you and hear your voice."

The deep emotion in his tone touched a chord inside her and that scared her almost more than his words. "Matt..."

He took her face in his hands and looked down into her eyes. "I just want to touch your hair and look at you in the moonlight," he said huskily, his gaze moving over her as though searching for something he couldn't name but needed badly.

She closed her eyes. His hands felt like heaven on her skin. This was so dangerous. What if she let herself fall in love with this man? Would she regret it forever?

"Matt, why are you doing this?" Sincerely troubled, she looked up at him.

He leaned over her, his gaze on her mouth. "I don't know, Annie. I'm telling myself not to, even now. But there is something pulling me back to you every time I try to break away."

"Matt…"

He kissed her softly. It wasn't like it had been before when they'd fallen under the passion spell. His kiss was soft, as though he cherished her, and she felt a glow from it. After they drew apart, he gave her a long, slow smile, tucked her hand into the crook of his arm, and they continued their walk along the brush-covered edge. She felt strangely light, as though she could dance out over the canyon if she wanted to.

They talked about general things—the preparations for the wedding, the weather, a new store opening downtown. And all the while she felt the glow, and finally she realized what it might be. Happiness. He'd made it clear that he needed her to help him heal the pain of the day. And that aroused warm feelings inside her. There was no way to guard against something like that.

"I found out what gender my baby is today," she told him as they turned back toward the house.

He smiled at her, clearly glad she'd finally done that. "Good. About time. So tell me, what is it?"

"He's a boy."

He nodded, squeezing her hand. "Great. What are you going to name him?"

"I don't know," she said evasively. "I'm avoiding that at the moment."

No name. That was a given. Once this baby had a name, she would never be able to hand him over to another mother.

Did kissing Matt do the same thing—cross a bridge that was hard to retreat from? If she kissed him too often would she fall in love? And if she was in love, would she be able to walk away?

That was just it. She had to give herself that freedom. She knew instinctively that she could depend on him for a lot of things, and that he would never leave her in the lurch the way Rick had. But she also knew that those bare essentials weren't enough. She might be making Matt happy right now, just being with him, but she knew that his feelings for her were based on her pregnancy. And that wasn't enough for her to let down her guard. She wanted it all. She wanted true love. And without it, she would never give up her freedom again.

It was a hot, windy Saturday afternoon and everyone was gone but Annie. Rita and Jodie had driven down to San Antonio to look for dresses for the wedding and David was off playing tennis with friends. Annie was restless.

Her baby was jumping around like a kid on a trampoline, making her laugh. She looked down the corridor. There was Matt's room. Something about it drew her in that direction.

Padding silently down the hall, she tried the knob. The door came open easily. Silently, she slipped into the room.

Just looking around at the pictures, books and personal items made her miss him. He hadn't been back again since the night he'd been so tortured and had seemed to need her to help lift his spirits. At work he was cool and professional. She couldn't tell what he was thinking. After the night they'd walked by the canyon, she'd thought he would be more affectionate in everyday life. But if anything, he was less so. To say she was confused would be to put it mildly.

But that was okay. Being confused was better than being in love.

Nothing had moved in this room since the night he'd packed up and left, just to make her feel more comfortable staying in his house. She picked up an old baseball lying on his shelf. It had an autograph of someone she didn't recognize. She was squinting at it when she thought she heard a board creak. Holding her breath, she listened. Nothing. She relaxed. This was an old house with numerous additions. It was going to creak.

Putting down the baseball, she looked at the picture of Matt's mother. She'd had a pretty face, calm with a sense of fun in her eyes. Losing your mother was always tough. It hadn't exactly been a bed of roses for her, and she'd been a grown woman. But to be a youngster and have your mother die had to be something you never did completely get over.

She sighed. Why was it that every time she thought

about Matt she either found something to sympathize with or something to admire? She had to stop this. Maybe she ought to ask his sisters to itemize some of his bad qualities, just to give her something to use to resist liking him too much.

Turning, she looked at the bed.

That bouncy bed. She smiled. Throwing her arms out, she let herself fall on it, giggling as it bounced. Then she lay still on her back, her hands on her belly, and closed her eyes, trying to catch Matt's scent in his bed. If only…

"So, what do you think you're doin' here, missy?"

The voice went through her like a jagged knife and she shot up to a sitting position. Jesse Allman stood in the doorway. That was who it had to be. Old and sick, he still had the power to scare her.

"N-n-nothing," she stammered.

"Do you know who I am?"

She nodded. "Yes, Mr. Allman. I think I do."

He glowered and pointed at her belly. "Did Matt do that?" he demanded.

She gasped. He certainly did come right to the point. "No, he did not," she told him, managing to sound as indignant as she felt.

"Good." He nodded. "There's been too much of that sort of thing going on around here."

She blinked at him. "There has?"

"Sure. Why I remember, back in the summer of '75…" He caught himself short and looked at her, then cleared his throat. "Well, never mind that." He looked at the evidence of her pregnancy again and shook his head disapprovingly. "I suppose you're not married."

"No, sir, I'm not." She raised her chin, just to let him know she wasn't as ashamed of that as he seemed to think she should be.

"And I suppose you're going to end up marrying Matt, aren't you?"

Her jaw dropped on that one. "No! There's no reason in the world I would marry Matt."

He gave her a scornful laugh. "Sure there is. I saw you a-lyin' there on his bed looking all dreamy and such."

She stood as though the bed had suddenly turned into a hot potato. No force on earth could have compelled her back to that bed now. "I was just…just…"

He waved her to silence. "Honey, I've been around for a long time. I've seen a lot of things. When you're young, you try to pretend you can overcome human nature. I'm here to tell you, your fight will be in vain. When you fall in love, that's all that matters to you and you'll knock over your best friend's mother to get to what you need."

Now she really was offended. "Oh, that's ridiculous."

"You mark my words, sweetie. I've been there. I've done wrong in my life. And I'm paying for it now. This old body has turned on me big time."

He stared at her, narrowing his eyes and squinting as he looked her over. "What did you say your name was?"

She hadn't, but she didn't want to be rude. "Annie Torres."

"Annie Torres, eh?" His mouth twisted in a grin that looked too cynical to be humorous. "Any relation to a little gal named Marina Torres? The one that used to be the housekeeper out at the McLaughlin place?"

She was so used to seeing no recognition in the faces around her she'd forgotten there was always the chance that someone would recognize who she was. Her heart sank and she thought fast. She could lie. But there really was no point, was there?

"She was my mother," she admitted at last.

He nodded, head cocked to the side. "She was a pretty little thing, just like you. How's she doin'?"

"She died last year."

"Oh. Well, I'm real sorry to hear that." He went back to studying her face. "So you're Marina's little girl."

She shivered, sure that he saw everything there was to see inside her, like an X ray.

"Yeah, okay. I see the resemblance."

The way he said it made her wonder what resemblance he was talking about. After all, he'd known both her parents—even if she hadn't. She looked at him sharply but his dark glittering eyes weren't revealing anything at all. Only moments later, his words said it all.

"You know who your daddy was?"

She couldn't help but react defensively. "Why? Do you?"

"Well, I can't say as I know it for sure, but your mother, Marina, she said it was William McLaughlin at the time. And we all figured she knew what she was talking about."

Annie nodded slowly. It took her breath away to have it confirmed like this. "That's what she told me, too."

"Them two McLaughlin boys, William and Richard, neither one of 'em was good for much." Obviously tiring, he looked around for support and pulled out the desk chair, sitting in it heavily. "Tell you one thing," he said. "We Allmans may have had the reputation for being the prairie scum of the town patriarchs, but I wasn't ever unfaithful to my Marie, not one time. Not in word, thought or deed. She was the light of my life. When I lost her, I thought I wanted to die, too. Instead, I built myself a business. Funny, isn't it? I guess a man's got to put his passion somewhere."

"I'm sure she would be proud of you," Annie said, then wondered why she had automatically wanted to comfort him. Strange.

"Sure," he said. "I was always prouder than a peacock of her. She was an angel. Did you know she probably saved your mother on her last night in town when the McLaughlins kicked her out?"

Annie's chest suddenly felt very tight. Reaching out, she sat back down on the bed. "What are you talking about?"

"My Marie found your mother shivering in Coyote Park in the dead of winter, pregnant and crying, with nowhere to go. She brought her home, fed her, made her up a bed on the couch. I remember how small and miserable she looked lying there. And the next day, Marie drove her all the way to San Antone to her brother's place."

"My uncle Jorge."

"That's the one. I guess he put her up until you were born."

"Yes."

"Well, she brought you by a couple of times over the years, when you were just a toddler. You wouldn't remember that. But then we didn't see any more of you and your mother. Marie used to wonder how you were doing. And now you're back here in the very same house where your mother was. Life is peculiar, no doubt about it."

He pulled himself out of the chair and left without another word. Annie stared after him, stunned by what she'd heard. She'd had no idea.

And then she realized she had to do something about this and do it fast.

Chapter Nine

Matt was sitting in a corner booth at the café, contemplating a meal of Millie's deluxe version of huevos rancheros with red salsa and black beans. He'd been out running at the high school track and this was the reward he gave himself for being so virtuous in the exercise department.

"Doesn't the meal kind of cancel out the benefits from the running?" Millie teased him, as usual.

"Haven't you ever heard the theory that strong muscles need to be fed?" he countered.

"I'll take your word for it. You do look like you know what you're talking about." She raised one eyebrow as she moved on to the next customer.

He looked down at the meal she'd put in front of him. It looked delicious, and he'd just begun piling the eggs onto the warm flour tortilla, anticipating how good it was going to taste, when Annie appeared out of nowhere, sinking into the seat across from him and sighing with relief.

"I'm so glad I found you here," she said, grabbing his glass of water and taking a long drink. "I'm dying of thirst."

She looked hot and tired, but still managed to be beautiful. He loved the way her hair curled wildly about her face. He loved how bright her dark eyes were, so interested in everything around her—the way her hands moved when she talked, the way…

He pulled himself up short. This was no time to let his feelings run away with him. She'd obviously come looking for him with a purpose in mind.

"What happened?" he asked.

"Oh, I had to walk all the way over here. My car broke down again and—"

"Damn it, Annie, I've told you to let me take that junker over to Al's Garage."

"No," she said sharply. "It's my responsibility. I'll take care of it."

He shrugged. It was on the tip of his tongue to point out that words weren't keeping the old heap from letting her down every other day, but he held it back. He knew how firmly she cherished her independence.

"So what's up?" he asked, positioning his fully stuffed tortilla for his first bite. "How did you know I was here?"

"I called Rafe's apartment and he said you might be here."

He paused, tortilla in the air. "Is something wrong?"

"Not exactly, but—" she hesitated, licking her lips "—I had an interview with your father."

The tortilla dropped back down onto his plate. "Oh, my God. What did he say? Did he do anything?"

"Well, first he wanted to know if you had done this." She looked down at her pregnant form.

Matt groaned.

"I told him no, that this baby had nothing to do with you."

Matt grinned. He could picture their encounter now. "Did that disappoint him?"

"No. I don't know." She shook her head, looking distracted. "That didn't really upset me." Reaching across the table, she put her hand on his. "But…oh, Matt, I feel like I need to be more honest with you. There's something I haven't told you. And now it's so late."

His heart went cold inside him. "What are you talking about, Annie?"

She shook her head and her face was full of misery. "I've been too scared to tell you," she began, then her eyes welled with tears. "It's going to be hard to explain."

"Okay," he said decisively, pushing his plate away. "Let's get out of here. Let's go somewhere where we can talk."

"But you just started eating," she protested.

"Forget it." He threw some money on the table, slid out of his seat and reached for her hand to help her out. "My car's right outside."

They walked out past the barbecue pit. A brand-new

shiny stainless steel grill was being erected by workmen in preparation for the Allman family prewedding party scheduled for Friday night. There was going to be Texas barbecue to die for. Matt opened the car door to help her in. He had no idea what she was about to reveal to him but he was pretty sure he wasn't going to like it. Still, he knew it wasn't going to change anything. He was crazy about her.

A few minutes later they were pulling up into a protected area off the highway, under a stand of junipers. Matt switched off the engine and turned to look at Annie. She'd settled down and was looking cool and composed now.

"You okay?" he asked.

She nodded. "Oh, yes, of course. Sorry I sort of fell apart there. That is so not me, but these pregnancy hormones keep undermining me."

He reached out and brushed a couple of wild curls back behind her shell-like ear. He couldn't help it. He just had to touch her.

"You said you had something to tell me?"

"Yes." Her gaze was troubled as it met his. "Your father recognized who I am. He knew my mother. And I think I should tell you before he does."

Alarm raised the hair on the back of his neck but he managed to stay outwardly calm. "Annie, I don't know what the hell you're talking about."

Taking a deep breath, she visibly set her shoulders and forced herself to speak. "Matt, my father was William McLaughlin. Josh and Kenny and Jimmy McLaughlin are all my half brothers."

He was usually pretty quick on the uptake but for some reason, this one had him stumped. "What?"

She folded her hands tightly together. "Remember when I told you that my mother fell in love with the young man of the family where she worked? She was working at McLaughlin Ranch at the time."

The fog began to clear. "You've got to be kidding. That means you're a McLaughlin."

"Yes." She closed her eyes as though she expected a torrent of anger from him.

He stared at her for a long moment, and then he started to laugh.

Her eyes popped open. "You're laughing?" she said indignantly. "You find this funny?"

He grabbed her hand and held it firmly in his. "Annie, I have to either laugh or cry. This is so bizarre. That you would turn out to be a member of the family I'm sworn as an Allman to hate forever… It's just too weird."

"Weird or not, it's true."

"And my father knew it?"

She nodded. "As soon as he heard my name, he recognized me. He told me about how your mother was the one who helped my mother get out of town when the McLaughlins kicked her out for being pregnant."

He shook his head. "It's a small world, isn't it?"

"And Chivaree was a small town back then."

"So that's why you felt this compulsion to keep going out to the McLaughlin Ranch." His gaze sharpened. "Do they know?"

She shook her head. "Cathy and Josh? No. I haven't

had the nerve to tell them yet. I wanted to get to know them before…"

He waited but she didn't complete the sentence.

"I don't get it. Why didn't you tell them from the beginning?"

She sighed, looking miserable. "That's what I'm asking myself now. I realize I should have. But I wanted to get the lay of the land and see what kind of people they were. I wanted to find out how they might accept that from me." She shook her head. "And now I'm wondering if I should even intrude on their happiness with my sad little tale. What does it really have to do with them?"

"Everything." He tugged on her hand. "Let's go and tell them. I'll go with you."

She shook her head, startled and resistant. "No! Not now." She looked confused. "Matt, they're such nice people. I like them so much. How can I just swoop down and ruin their picture of their father like that?"

"Don't worry about that," he said grimly. "Everyone knows Josh's father was a playboy. It's common knowledge around town." Too late, he realized he was talking about her father, too.

But it didn't seem to bother her. "I know that," she said. "But to confront them with it so directly seems cruel. Maybe we can just let this die down." She looked at him hopefully.

He shook his head. "You have to tell them. My father knows and he won't keep your secret for long."

She seemed so miserable, his heart went out to her and he leaned forward and dropped a tender kiss on her lips. She turned toward him as though he'd done something special and he was tempted to take things a little further. But he resisted. She was torn and weak now and it was no time to push it.

"Come on," he said. "I'll drive you over and go in with you."

Her sigh seemed to come from deep inside her. "All right," she said softly, but she looked as though she was going to her doom.

"What do you want?"

Josh had looked happy enough to see Annie, but when he caught sight of Matt standing behind her, his face changed. Now he stood squarely in the opening, not leaving any room for entrance.

"I need to tell you something," Annie said, her pulse pounding. "Can we come in?"

"*You* can come in," Josh said, staring coldly at Matt. "But I'd rather he stayed out here."

Cathy had come up behind him by now and she was appalled at his attitude.

"Josh McLaughlin, you will not leave our guests standing out on the porch." She gave him a push to get him out of the way and smiled out at them. "Please. Won't you both come inside?"

They did so and Emily ran straight for Annie with a cry of joy. Annie curled the child into her arms and kissed her cheek, then set her down and turned back to face Josh who was glowering darkly.

"Won't you sit down?" Cathy offered.

Annie shook her head. "Thanks, but we won't be here long. I've just got something I have to tell you. It's a hard thing to do, and I'm afraid you're going to be very angry. And you have every right to be."

Cathy looked alarmed and took Emily up in her arms, carting her off to her playroom, then returning without her.

"Josh… Cathy…" Annie made a gesture almost of supplication with both hands. "I've been coming to your house under false pretenses."

"What are you talking about?" Josh demanded.

"I… uh…" Words stuck in her throat and she licked her dry lips. How could she do this? She looked at Matt. He looked like he might step forward and do the talking if she didn't hurry up and take care of it herself. Turning back, she steeled herself to the task.

"First I want to tell you both how much I love coming here and how welcome you've made me. I never would have dreamed you would turn out to be such a wonderful couple. I think the world of you. And Emily…" Her voice choked and she fought back the tears.

"Annie, what are you trying to say?"

"I never told you that my father was from Chivaree and that I partly grew up here. I never really knew him, though I did see him around town a few times when I was young."

She swallowed hard and glanced at Josh. From the look on his face she could see that he was withdrawing from her. The warmth was completely gone now. Was he beginning to realize what this was about?

"You see, my mother once worked here at McLaughlin Ranch. As a live-in housekeeper. And she fell in love with…with your father."

Josh groaned, turning away.

"I think you probably know where I'm going with this," she said quickly. "Your father was my father, too." She looked up at him.

But Josh was glaring at Matt. "Did he put you up to this?" he demanded.

"No! He didn't know anything about it until today."

"Look, this really has nothing to do with me," Matt said firmly. "I'm just here to support Annie. That's all I care about."

"He encouraged me to come and tell you. To get it over with."

Josh looked completely unconvinced. "Okay, wait a minute. This is all just a little too convenient. You come to town and start living with the Allmans, and all of a sudden, you've got a claim on the McLaughlin estate?"

Annie eyes opened wide in horror. "I'm not making any claim."

"What do you call this? Of course you are."

"No!"

"Then why are you here?"

Words failed her. Why was she here? She stared at him mutely. How could she possibly explain the loneliness she'd felt? The need for connection?

"I didn't come here to get anything from you, Josh," she said at last. "And I don't have any grievance against you. The only person I could possibly have a grievance against would be our father if he was still alive. But he isn't. And you didn't have anything to do with what happened, any more than I did."

Matt stepped forward to help out. "Look, she's come

to tell you and that's that. If you need proof of what she's saying, we can have a DNA test done right away. It'll take about a week to get the results."

Josh sneered. "Why should I trust your DNA test?"

Matt grimaced. "Fine. Call in anyone you like. Listen, I hope she turns out to be wrong. I don't want her to be a McLaughlin." He sneered right back. "And anyway, she doesn't need you to take care of her. We'll take care of her."

Josh glared at him. "If she's really a McLaughlin, *we'll* take care of her."

Annie stepped between them, angry at them both now. "Nobody needs to take care of me. I can take care of myself!"

"Annie…"

They both said it at the same time, but she turned to Matt.

"Please, Matt. I appreciate your support, but your being here is just confusing the issue. I wish you'd wait outside for a minute."

That shocked him but he quickly realized she was right. He and Josh would be at loggerheads no matter what. "Okay. I'll go outside on the porch while you talk. You give a holler if you need me."

"I will."

Matt stood out on the porch, swearing softly to himself and trying to calm down. What was it about the McLaughlins that always got his back up no matter how much he tried to avoid it? Now here he was out on the McLaughlin Ranch for the first time ever. He'd lived in Chivaree most all his life and he'd never been to the biggest ranch in the territory.

It looked like rumors were true, anyway. Josh was fixing the place up. It looked pretty good. From what he'd heard it had been a wreck just a few short years ago when William had died. The older McLaughlin had been considered a loser as far as ranching was concerned. He was pretty good at running off to New York and dating showgirls, but ranching hadn't really been his line. The McLaughlins were lucky Josh had figured out how to do it right before they lost the whole operation.

A movement from the window caught his eye. He turned. A little face surrounded by bouncing auburn curls was peering out at him. He'd seen the little girl in the house when they'd first entered, but Cathy had whisked her away. Now she was back and grinning at him through the glass.

What a little sweetheart. He grinned back at her. She stuck out her tongue at him and he made a monster face in return. Throwing back her head, she laughed with delight. And darned if he didn't, too.

What a darling. He fell in love with her immediately and it made him ache to find his own child.

Then Annie was coming out the door, hurrying toward the car. "Let's go," she said.

He caught up with her in two quick strides and helped her into the seat, then went to the driver's side. In another moment they were back on the highway.

"You've been crying," he said after glancing her way and noting the tearful evidence. "He didn't hurt you, did he?"

"No, of course not." She sighed. "It's just the darn

old hormones. I swear, once this baby comes, I'm never going to cry again."

He laughed. "Oh, sweetie, from what I've heard about raising kids, the crying has only just begun."

She looked at him mutely. She wasn't going to pretend any longer that she was sure she was going to put this baby up for adoption.

"So what happened?" he said. "Did you get that jackass to calm down and listen?"

She stared at him for a long moment, then she started to smile. "That's my half brother you're talking about," she reminded him. "Though whether he's ever going to admit it, I don't know." Shaking her head, she looked out her window at the passing fence posts. "But that's not important, I guess. I told him what I had to tell him. If he wants to have any sort of relationship, that's up to him. I've done my part. And I'm going to stop worrying about it."

Easier said than done, she knew, but at least this was a step in the right direction.

She didn't think she could face the others right now so she was glad when Matt suggested they go to dinner at a steak place out on the interstate where they weren't likely to run into anyone they knew. They ate filet mignon that melted in their mouths and lingered over crème brûlée for dessert. Matt kept the evening light, telling stories about how he and his brothers used to put gray hair on their parents' heads with their antics through the years. Annie laughed more than she'd laughed in years and told a few stories of her own.

It was late by the time they headed back. When they

reached the Allman house, Matt pulled the car to the side under the trees and shut off the engine and the lights, then turned to her instead of getting out.

Watching her tonight, he'd tried to remember why he'd decided that he couldn't fall in love with her. Whatever those reasons were, they were gone now, and the ones he could remember didn't seem to make sense anymore. She'd filled his life with sunlight over the past few weeks and he couldn't imagine going on without her.

"Annie," he said, leaning toward her and taking her hands in his, "I don't want to leave you here. I want to take you with me. I want to fall asleep with you curled up against me. I want..."

She kissed him passionately, mostly to stop whatever he was about to say, and then his arms were around her and he was gathering her to him. And she wanted to go with him. She wanted to be in his arms more than she wanted anything.

She moaned as she arched against him. Her breasts felt full and when he cupped them, she gasped at how wonderful his touch was. He pushed away the fabric of her shirt, then the lace of her bra, and she was fully exposed to his caress.

"Annie, Annie," he breathed against her breast. "You make me crazy."

She knew that feeling. Her hand slid underneath his shirt, molding the hard muscles of his chest, the tight nipple, the light sprinkling of wiry hair. She wanted to follow her hand with her mouth, her tongue. She wanted to touch every part of him, to taste him, too.

And then a surge of sensation came over her and she knew that she wanted much more than that. She wanted to make love to this man, needed him almost as much as she needed to breathe. And if she didn't exert a little self-control, things were going to get way out of hand.

"Stop," she said, but he didn't seem to hear her. His tongue was traveling down to the tip of her breast and she was going to go mad if he didn't stop. "Matt, stop," she cried, pushing as hard as she could to get his attention.

He groaned, drawing back and catching his breath. He watched as she pulled her clothes together. "You are so beautiful," he said huskily. "You can wrap me around your little finger anytime."

She gave him a mischievous smile. "I'll keep that in mind."

"Annie." He sat up straighter and got serious. "I was thinking. You know what? Maybe we should get married."

"What?"

Her reaction wasn't quite what he'd hoped.

"Well, why not? We like each other pretty well and you need a husband."

She stared at him in the darkness of the car. How lovely it would be to relax and let herself believe that would solve everything.

The only reason he says he wants to marry you is to help you and to make sure you don't give your baby up for adoption, she reminded herself. *It's not like he loves you. He hasn't said a word about love.*

She turned from him. "I'm never getting married," she murmured.

"What are you talking about?"

"My life. Thanks for the dinner, Matt. Good night." She opened the car door and was off up the path to the house like a flash. Anyone watching would hardly be able to believe that she was almost eight months pregnant.

Matt watched her go, frowning and wondering if he was ever going to be able to understand her.

It didn't take long to find out the answer to Annie's question as to whether or not Josh was interested in pursuing a family connection. In fact, family relationships seemed to be breaking out all over.

The wedding was less than two weeks away and that very morning, Kurt and Jodie had announced that they had decided to make it a double wedding with Shelley and Rafe.

"We just can't wait any longer," Jodie had told her beaming family. "Katy needs us to be an official family and we've decided that's more important than trying not to hurt the feelings of people who aren't even here."

She was talking about Kurt's mother who was in New York and his sister, Tracy, who was with her latest fiancé in Dallas. Meanwhile, his father was still somewhere in Europe and no one had heard from him in months. None of these family members showed any signs of ever coming back to Chivaree.

"I've got a couple of uncles hanging around," Kurt added. "But I'm not close to any of them. The only cousin I would like to have come would be Josh. Maybe we'll send him an invitation and see if he's got the guts to brave the feud."

Rita had tears in her eyes. "I'm so glad," she said, hugging them both. "This is going to be the most wonderful wedding ever."

Annie had been happy for them all, but the comment about Josh had hit home. She was pretty sure she'd sabotaged any hope they had of getting that branch of the McLaughlins to come to the wedding. Looking up, she'd met Matt's gaze and knew he was thinking the same thing.

Later that day, she was working on a scheduling problem and had papers set in piles all over her desk when she sensed someone in the doorway. Turning, she found herself face-to-face with Josh.

"Oh!" she said, one hand going to her mouth in surprise.

"Hi," he said. His eyes were dark and troubled. "I guess we'd better talk."

Chapter Ten

Matt was there, supporting her with an arm around her waist, before she had time to turn and look for him.

"How about we take this to the boardroom?" he suggested quietly. "That way you two won't be disturbed."

They took the ancient elevator. As the three of them stood in the swaying car as it creaked its way to the boardroom floor, Annie realized she was standing between the two men she cared for most in the world. She said a quick prayer that they would both still care for her when all this was over.

The recently remodeled boardroom had a hushed atmosphere, as if only important things should happen there. One wall was lined with impressively ornate bookcases full of beautifully bound volumes while the other was paneled in elegant mahogany and decorated with framed awards the company had won. The table was long and heavy and the chairs that lined it were richly upholstered.

"Would you like me to wait outside?" Matt asked, turning toward Annie, but looking at Josh.

Josh shook his head. "No, you might as well stay."

The three of them slipped into chairs at one end of the table. Josh leaned forward, his gaze on Annie.

"I want to tell you right up front that I've talked to some old-timers who back your story all the way. In fact, Hiram, who's been our head wrangler for thirty years, said he knew who you were the moment he saw you."

Annie breathed again. It was such a relief to have him believe her. "Why didn't he say anything?" she asked.

Josh shrugged. "He said 'it weren't none of his business' and he thought we would work it out ourselves. I hope we can do that."

She nodded. "Oh, yes."

"I've got to ask you one question that is still bothering me. What exactly did you come here for?"

Very quickly she explained to him about what had happened with her mother. She went right on into her own experience with Rick, talking quickly, getting it over with and hoping she would never have to go into it again. But she wanted him to know how lost and alone she'd felt, how she'd longed for a family, even a distant one.

"My mother was dead. My uncle had moved back to Mexico long ago and hadn't been heard from since. Chivaree was always my only home. I didn't know where else to go. And since you are the only family I felt I had in the world, I wanted to make contact. When I saw your ad, it felt like an answer to a prayer."

His eyes were still troubled. "Why didn't you approach us directly?"

"I didn't know if I really wanted to do that. I thought I ought to get to know you first. I really didn't want to create a problem. And actually, I'd about decided I wasn't going to tell you after all, but someone recognized me and I knew it would get to you eventually. So Matt finally convinced me that I'd better go ahead and tell you." She shook her head. "Now I realize it would have been better to tell you from the first. I'm sorry. I never meant to hurt anyone."

He stared at his own folded hands for a long moment, then looked up. "I guess we need to negotiate some kind of settlement for you."

"Settlement?" She was horrified. "I don't want a settlement. I don't want a penny from you." She rose from her seat, so determined to convince him. "Really, Josh. Not a penny."

He rose as well and looked at her. "Okay, Annie. But how about a little love?" And suddenly he opened his arms. "Please. Be part of our family."

With a cry, she flew into his arms and he held her tightly, looking over her head at Matt, then back down at her dark hair. "Cathy misses you. How about coming to dinner Wednesday night?"

"I'd love to," she said, her eyes shining with happiness.

"And why don't you bring him along?" Josh said, gesturing toward Matt. "I have a feeling that we might as well get to know him, too."

The dinner went beautifully. After a wary start, Josh and Matt found more and more things in common, and by the time Annie and Matt said good night, the men were both close to admitting they could actually become good friends if they tried. In fact, things seemed to be going so smoothly, Annie felt bold enough to ask if they had received the wedding invitation from Jodie and Kurt.

"We'll be there," Cathy told her, laughing. "With bells on."

"Do you think the great Allman-McLaughlin feud is finally going to crumble?" Annie asked hopefully.

"No crumbling just yet," Josh warned. He exchanged glances with Matt. "But a few major cracks are definitely appearing."

Matt got so enthused he invited them to the family prewedding dinner at Millie's the next night. And they agreed to come to that, too.

Driving home, Annie was in heaven.

"William," she said, loud and clear, like a royal pronouncement.

"What?" Matt looked over at her in surprise.

"William. I'm going to name my baby William. After my father."

He nodded, his eyes on the road, and a slow smile grew on his handsome face. "We'll call him Billy," he said. "I'll teach him how to ride and how to throw a fast ball." He glanced at her. "He can call me Uncle Matt."

She nodded happily. "You've got a deal," she told him.

"Or…" He pulled into the driveway and turned off the engine, then reached for her. "He could call me Dad. It's up to you."

She didn't answer, losing herself in his kiss. For the

first time, she dared to open up and give him clear evidence of what she felt for him. This time it wasn't laced with the driving physical hunger she'd had in the past. It was much more than that, much deeper, much more important. Could he tell that she was in love?

Maybe. Maybe not. But he kissed her with the same cherishing emotion. And when he pulled back, his smile was loving, even if he didn't say the words. But what he did say was pretty good.

"You are the best thing in my life right now."

Her heart skipped. "You too? I thought I was the only one."

He grinned and chucked her under the chin, then thought of something else. "The second best part of the evening was getting to see that adorable little girl again. How old is she?"

"Emily? About eighteen months."

"That's what I thought. Probably about the same age as my baby should be."

"Yes, that's right."

"Looking at her I was thinking that my baby might look very similar."

"Yes, very likely."

She was about to point out that Emily was adopted, just to score another point or two on his arguments, when a realization hit her like a thunderbolt. And once it had hit, she couldn't believe she hadn't thought of it before.

Her heart began to beat very fast. The things he'd told her about his baby—how his girlfriend had given birth in San Antonio and then possibly given up the baby for adoption, how the private detective was searching for a filing out of state—came back to her. Cathy had said they had adopted Emily privately in San Antonio and that Emily's birth mother requested someone from Chivaree, but that they'd had to file over the border to expedite things.

Surely there couldn't be a connection. Could there? No, that would be too much of a coincidence. Wouldn't it?

The night was long and lonely when sleep wouldn't come. Annie spent most of it at her bedroom window, looking out at the moon. What was she going to do?

The more she thought about it the more she was afraid it was a very good possibility that Emily was Matt's biological child. On the one hand, that would end Matt's desperate search. On the other, that was sure to destroy the wonderful new relationship between Matt and Josh—not to mention hers with them both. Would there be a court case? Would Matt insist on asserting his parental rights? Knowing Matt as she did, knowing his passion to find his child, she was afraid he would. And she knew Josh and Cathy would fight that tooth and nail.

Of course, she had to tell Matt what she suspected. And if she'd learned anything over the last few weeks, sooner would be better than later. In fact, she wished she'd gone ahead and told him the moment she thought of it. Well, she would tell him first thing in the office. And though she dreaded what was going to happen next, it would be a relief to get it off her chest.

Unfortunately, quick relief was not to be. Once in the office she found a message from Matt. A drug he needed for one of his private patients was stuck in a mail room in San Antonio and he was on his way to pick it up personally. He would be with his patient all afternoon and wouldn't see her until that evening at Millie's.

Annie worked all day with the apprehension of what was next hanging over her. To add to the misery, by afternoon she was feeling strange, sort of depressed and unsettled. She began to think that maybe she wouldn't tell him until after the party was over. After all, with Josh and Cathy sitting there in Millie's, just starting to get to know the Allmans, how could she ruin it all?

She was preparing to leave the office and head over to the café when Matt's private line rang in his office. She was only half listening to the message being left on his answering machine when she realized who it was.

"Hey, Matt. It's Dan Kramer. I've got good news. I found your baby. And the wacky thing is, she was adopted by a couple right there in the same town where you live. I'll try to catch you on your cell, or at your brother's apartment, but in case I don't, call me back. Later."

She stood frozen to the spot, unable to breathe. It was true, then. It was true and she hadn't told him. He wasn't going to forgive her for that. She had to find him right away. Maybe he was already at Millie's.

She raced over, nursing her sick car, which just barely chugged to life. Millie's was already filling up. The Allmans had taken it over for the night and relatives were driving in from all over the county. Searching quickly, she didn't see Matt at first, but there were Josh and Cathy waving to her from a booth, Emily sitting between them. She waved back, trying not to look as stricken as she felt, and then she saw Matt. He saw her and his eyes lit up. But just as he started toward her, Rafe stopped him and she could just make out what he was saying.

"Hey, Matt, that private eye called just before I left the apartment. He's got news and wants you to call him right away."

Matt turned toward the telephone and Annie's heart sank. That was it. Now he would know. She'd made such a mess of everything. Would he go right up to Josh and Cathy and tell them? Was it fair for her not to warn them? But wouldn't it be a betrayal to Matt if she did? Would they gather Emily up in their arms and head for home to call their lawyer? Would Matt want to know why Annie hadn't told him what she knew?

She felt light-headed, as though she might faint right here in the middle of Millie's again.

"Hey, honey," Millie said. "Are you okay?"

She grabbed Millie's hand. "He'll never understand," she muttered, looking at her wildly. "I should have told him sooner. It's all going to fall apart and it's all my fault."

Turning blindly, she headed for the door. She had to get out of there. Houston was looking good. Could she make it by midnight?

Once the contractions really got going she realized that the odd, queasy, achy way she'd been feeling all afternoon had been her body setting the stage for the big event. She just hadn't paid enough attention to realize what was going on. After all, her due date wasn't for a few weeks yet.

One thing was for sure—she wasn't going to make it to Houston. She wasn't even going to make it to Austin.

In fact, she was lucky she'd made it to Coyote Park before her car died. She'd only meant to drive by the place, just one last look in tribute to her past. But by the time she got there, her car was sputtering. She pulled into the parking lot just in time to hear the death rattle. The car had stopped and it just wasn't going to go anymore. No matter what she did she wasn't going to get it started again.

So here she was with no car, no cell phone, no nothing. The park was dark and empty. There was no sign of another human being for miles. And she was going into labor.

She wasted a couple of minutes in disbelieving anguish, then got down to work. She needed a good, clean place to have her baby. She went quickly to the building that housed the bathrooms and the meeting room. The bathrooms were open and relatively clean, but the meeting room was locked.

"It's a good thing I grew up in this park," she said. As she remembered, there used to be an extra key hidden above the door. Pulling over an old plastic milk crate, she used it to climb up and feel behind the top brick on the right. Sure enough, the key was still there.

"After all these years," she muttered to herself, amazed and thankful.

She unlocked the door and went inside. It looked very much the same as it had in her childhood, with floor-to-ceiling cupboards holding crafts supplies on one side of the room and a stack of folding chairs along with a long worktable on the other. The electricity worked. There was even a sink with running water. Luckily, someone was keeping it all clean. Making her way back out to the car, she had to stop and do the breathing she'd learned in nursing school while a contraction hardened her belly like a rock before she could move on to collect part of a pile of clothes she kept in the trunk. Gathering them up in her arms, she went back to the meeting room and began making a nest for herself in the corner.

She'd also picked up a pad of paper and a pen and she began writing down her contractions, using the time on her watch. To her surprise, a lot of her nursing training was coming back to her and she began to feel confident. She could do this.

"Pioneer women did this all the time," she told herself bracingly. "And they didn't have any nursing experience."

One hour went by. She got herself a drink of water and tried to walk during the contractions. Another hour went by, and now walking was not an option. It was dark outside, but the single bulb in the center of the room was keeping out the night. She wondered if anyone would see the light from the highway and come down to investigate. She wondered what Matt was doing right now. And what he was thinking.

She couldn't believe she'd muddled things up so badly. If only she'd been up front with everyone about everything right from the first, she probably wouldn't be in this predicament.

"Oh, Billy-boy," she said breathlessly as another contraction took over. They were getting overwhelming now. She was actually moaning, something she'd sworn she wouldn't do. And a little bit of doubt as to whether she could pull this off was creeping in. But when the need to push came, she was ready to give it her all. Once the baby started coming, she wanted him out and breathing as fast as possible.

"Oh!"

This contraction was like a vise. She was puffing away at the breathing and it wasn't doing any good at all. She wasn't sure she could handle this. It ended but another one started before she had time to catch her breath, and this one was even worse. She couldn't take it.

"Oh, Matt!" she cried out in despair.

And then, like a miracle, he was there.

"Annie, Annie, my sweet Annie." He took over, examining her dilation at the same time he whipped out his cell phone and barked into it with directions for an ambulance. "Just hold on, darling. I know you're going to want to push. Try to hold it back until I can get you ready."

Hold it back! That would be like telling the earth to hold off on that next rotation thing. Nothing was holding this baby back. He was coming now!

But she did manage to put him off for a couple of contractions, much to her own amazement.

"I can't," she told Matt, panting as the second one diminished for a moment. "I can't!"

"You're doing beautifully, Annie. We've got the head crowned." He put a hand on her belly and nodded. "Here comes another one. You can push this time, Annie. I'm ready for him."

She pushed with a growl that must have shaken the walls of the place.

"Okay, we've got the head. One more push."

She gave it everything she had left and felt the baby sliding out into the world.

"Here he is," Matt said joyfully. He held him up where she could see. He was long and stretched and covered with white stuff and the most beautiful thing she'd ever seen. "Meet Mr. William."

"Billy," she reminded him weakly, reaching out to touch his tiny fingers. Pride and joy burst inside her. "Billy Matthew Torres."

He grinned at her. "Are you sure?"

"I'm sure."

He leaned down and kissed her. She wanted to respond but she was just too tired. Still, she was drowning in happiness.

"How did you get here? How did you know?"

"It took awhile. Much too long. Everything was so confused. I didn't know you'd taken off until Millie told me. Then I started to worry. I went back to the house looking for you. When you weren't there, I started to get crazy. And then I remembered the attachment you had to this park, and I came here."

She could hear the siren coming. The ambulance was here. The image of her newborn baby was imprinted on her brain and she didn't want to see anything else. Closing her eyes, she slept.

She woke up in a hospital room. Matt was sitting beside the bed, waiting for her to come back from dreamland. She smiled at him.

"I have a baby," she said with groggy wonder.

"Yes, you do," he said, reaching out to take her hand in his. "You turned out to be a champ at this baby-delivery thing."

"Did I?"

"First class. And you produced one great baby. Eight pounds, four ounces, ready to rumble."

She laughed, then stopped herself. "Ouch. I'm really sore."

"No wonder. You ran a marathon last night, Annie. And you won the race."

She closed her eyes as it all flooded back to her—Emily, Josh and Cathy, the feud.

"Are you mad at me?" she asked him.

"Actually, I'm furious with you."

Her eyes snapped open and she stared at him. "Really?"

"Yes. For many things." He kissed her fingers. "But they might not be what you think they are."

"What, then? Tell me."

"Okay. First, I'm really ticked off about you running into the night without telling anyone where you were going. You got yourself into a very dangerous situation. That was just plain crazy."

"You know, I was a little crazy last night. I guess it was going into labor and all. I didn't think straight. But you're right. I'm very sorry." She looked contrite for a moment, then gave it up. "What else?"

"Okay. The other thing I'm angry about is that you had so little faith in me."

"What do you mean?"

"Annie…" He raised her fingers to his lips again. "What did you think I was going to do when I found out about Emily?"

She didn't answer. He waited a moment, then went on.

"Annie, Annie, how could you think I would be prepared to rip that family apart? I would be harming my own baby if I did that. I was obsessed with finding her in order to make sure she was okay. Unless I found her in some sort of distress, I never planned to try to gain custody just for my own selfish needs if she was in a good family situation. How could I do a thing like that? But I had to see for myself that she was thriving."

"Of course." She frowned, looking at him searchingly. "Then you're not going to try to get custody?"

"No. Josh and Cathy and I went head-on right there at Millie's. In fact, if it hadn't been for that, I would have found you sooner. They were shocked at first, shocked and a little scared. But I reassured them right away. We'll be working out more of the details over the next few days." He dropped a kiss into her palm. "All I want is to be able to be a part of her life. I'll be her uncle Matt. It'll all work out." He smiled down at her. "And it will work out even better once we get married."

"Married? Wait a minute…"

"No, Annie. I'm not waiting any longer." He cupped her cheek with one hand. "I love you. I want to marry you. Billy needs a dad, you need a husband—and I need a lover."

But Annie hadn't heard anything beyond his third sentence. "You love me?" she asked in a quavering voice, just wanting to be sure.

"Oh, God, woman, couldn't you tell? I thought females were the intuitive ones who knew all this stuff. Yes, I love you. I've loved you since the first moment you threw yourself at my feet."

"Well, guess what," she came back at him, shimmering with joy. "I've loved you ever since that day you tripped me in Millie's. When you picked me up and carried me out of there, I fell head over heels. I've always wanted a caveman for a husband."

"Then you'll marry me?"

"Do I have any choice?"

He laughed. "No," he said as he bent down to kiss her lips. "No choice at all."

Epilogue

The wedding day arrived and all the hard work paid off stunningly. The Allmans' yard looked like a magical land. Flower garlands were strung from the trees, white birdcages filled with white doves hung from posts, and the wedding cake on the patio table looked as big as the house. Three wedding arches stood at the end of the yard, each sporting a different color climbing rose. White wooden chairs were set out for the assembly. And the place was packed with people.

On a large chair, Jesse Allman sat waiting. In his mind he was going over the history of his family—and the McLaughlin family, too. He thought about the early days when his grandfather Hiram and Theodore McLaughlin founded the town of Chivaree and were partners until Theodore kidnapped Jesse's grandmother and tried to seduce her. To get her back, Hiram had to gather enough men and weapons to storm the ranch house where Theodore was holding her. That had been before his time, but he remembered—as though it was just weeks ago—the day his own father, Hank Allman, found out Calvin McLaughlin had stolen the lease to his good bottom land out on the Bandito River and there was no way he could prove it. Then there were the everyday fights, including the time William and Richard McLaughlin had tied Jesse himself to a post in front of the city hall in his underwear for everyone in town to see and laugh at. And the times his own boys had been harassed by that scummy crew. Not to mention the better times when the Allmans had found ways to get the McLaughlins back.

Over the years he'd developed a grudge against just about every McLaughlin there was for having done something bad to someone in his family. And the more he thought back over all those incidents, the more he grinned. Where were all those people now? William was dead. Richard was hiding out overseas. And the others were scattered here and there. Only a few McLaughlins still lived in Chivaree, and the good ones of those were coming more and more under Allman influence.

"Ready, Pop?"

"Ready as I'll ever be."

David had come to help him get to the proper placement. He let his son assist him to his feet and guide him into position. The people were all sitting in the white wooden chairs. The minister was standing between the three arbors. The music started up, the assembly rose and the three brides started coming out of the house, one by one, each looking beautiful in a lacy white gown.

He smiled at them all. The smiles he got in return were dazzling. He offered his daughter his arm and she slipped her hand in. Then he noticed Josh McLaughlin and Millie had joined them. The minister gave a short prayer and it was time to begin.

"Who gives this woman, Annie Torres, to be married to Matthew Allman?"

"Her brother, Josh McLaughlin," was the answer. Annie beamed at him as he presented her to Matt, who stood waiting.

"Who gives this woman, Shelley Sinclair, to be married to Raphael Allman?"

Millie stepped forward. "Her mother does," she said simply, kissing her daughter on the cheek before withdrawing.

"Who gives this woman, Jodie Allman, to be married to Kurt McLaughlin?"

It was Jesse's turn. "That would be me," he said, stepping forward proudly, presenting his beloved daughter to the world as he escorted her to Kurt's side. "Me and my Marie up in heaven." Jodie left him, but he wasn't finished. "Hey, Marie and me are giving our two boys, too, Matt and Rafe. Just so y'all don't forget."

"Pop!" all his children snapped at him at once.

"Oh, all right," he grumbled, heading back for his big chair.

The ceremony was over soon and the couples were kissing. The doves were released and they hovered around nicely before flying off. Celebration was in the air.

"We done it, Marie," Jesse whispered, looking up toward the bright blue sky. "We done it good. Gol'darn if we didn't go and win the feud."

* * * * *

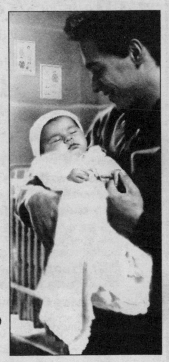